DANCE ON ICE

Chesterford Coyotes 3

RJ SCOTT

V.L. LOCEY

Love Lane Books

Copyright

Dance on Ice

For the figure skater and the hockey player, their sport demands total devotion, but can falling in love come first?

My name is Shaun Stanton, and I'm bisexual.

In hockey-obsessed Chesterford Academy, Shaun Stanton stands out as the star player and captain of the Chesterford Coyotes, and his exceptional skills have already attracted the attention of NHL scouts. He lives and breathes hockey, but there's more to his story. His father wants Shaun to be the star he never was, and their relationship is a complex mix of guidance and intimidation. Worse, while hockey is Shaun's sanctuary and a key part of who he is, he harbors a secret his dad can never discover: Shaun is gay He's caught between the future career he's destined for, and the truth he has to hide. There's one bright light in his life, the vibrant figure skater who shares the early morning practice ice, a friend he worries about, but has now become something more —Kenji is everything Shaun wants and can't have.

My name is Kenji Kelly, and I need to be perfect.

Kenji Kelly is a young man who walks two worlds: his family is a beautiful mix of American and Asian cultures. He loves both figure skating and hockey, and he's an out and proud pansexual teen. While it seems to the world around him he has it all, deep down Kenji has a secret that's slowly becoming harder to conceal. His life is the ice and his coach does not believe in failure. The one person who knows his hidden secret is Shaun, the captain of the Coyotes and a friend from youth hockey days. Shaun's gaze towards Kenji, once filled with concern, now seems to hold something deeper, unsettling Kenji but also igniting similar giddy, burgeoning feelings in him. As their feelings for each other become stronger, the secrets both young men carry grow heavier and more distressing with each passing day.

———————

Trigger warning for eating disorder

Dedication

To my family who accepts me and all my foibles and quirks. Even the plastic banana in my holster.

VL Locey

Always for my family.

RJ Scott

Chapter One

Shaun

It's easy to put someone out of your mind if you don't see them.

But Kenji was there, and I stared like an idiot at the apparition, in a lilac T-shirt over tight leggings, as he skated onto the ice at the opposite end of the rink from me. For a moment, all my old instincts kicked in and all this fizzing joy filled me. I'd missed him so much. He was different, thinner than I remembered, almost fragile, but he was still the same Kenji Kelly, who made me smile. The sight of him sent a pang of guilt through me, a sharp reminder of the friendship

I'd thrown away, but he was the boy I'd grown up with, played peewee hockey with, and he was here, at my school, sharing the state-of-the-art rink that I'd always had to myself at six a.m.

What is he doing here?

I wondered if it was only me who could see him, but then Dad exploded. "Is that the freaking twirling kid that used to follow you around?" He snapped loud enough that Kenji and the man with him would hear. There was so much wrong with that statement, not the least of which was the hate dripping from Dad's words, the implication that being a figure skater meant Kenji was somehow *less*. I burned with embarrassment.

Kenji, turn and look at me… smile… Kenji! Hi!

I bit back on calling his name, and not once did Kenji glance over at either of us, although his coach met my dad's shocked reaction with his hands on his hips.

"I'm gonna find out what's going on!" Dad added a muttered curse word, then stalked around the rink to the coach and Kenji.

There was a heated exchange of words, Kenji skating backward and away, almost at center ice. All I needed to do was to push forward on one skate and glide there, and we could say hello. We'd been best friends once, and if I apologized—if I was honest with him about how I'd messed up—maybe we could go back to being friends. As the argument escalated between my dad and Kenji's coach, I felt a knot form in my stomach, and I was paralyzed by my own insecurities. I watched Kenji and cursed myself for not having the courage to reach out to him.

Dad was becoming more animated, Kenji's coach just as loud, gesticulating wildly.

I didn't have the balls to skate to the center ice.

And Kenji didn't turn to look at me.

Dad returned, as scarlet as me, but where my reaction was shame and confusion, his was temper and hatred.

"You're sharing the ice," he snapped.

He was so angry, and I didn't know how to feel. He'd sacrificed everything for me; worked three jobs to keep me in hockey gear, drove me to every practice and game, and even volunteered as a coach for the team. The thought of letting him down filled me with guilt.

I owed him.

He'd poured his heart and soul into my hockey career, and it all centered on us practicing six days out of seven on this ice, and today, we didn't have the ice.

I should feel territorial, right? It was what Dad

wanted me to feel, I was sure. Instead, I felt... weird. Then, something hit me. Why was I sharing the ice that was for the school? It was somewhere for the Academy teams to practice and play, and it wasn't open to the public, courtesy of a shit ton of funding from very rich benefactors at our very wealthy campus. Why was someone from outside Chesterford Academy on our ice?

"They'll let anyone join this damn school, freaking twirly shit getting in our way. Fucking prancing kids out here on our ice."

"He's—"

"No!"

I wanted to defend Kenji, to explain that figure skaters were as valid as hockey players, same as I'd done when Kenji had left hockey for figure skating, and I'd begged to be allowed to be friends with him still. But my dad's hatred had spilled over and scared me.

"Shut your mouth and listen up," Dad snapped. His reaction stung; his threats left me feeling powerless and defeated, and small.

So small.

"Figure skaters are boys as well," I word-vomited, thankful the boards were between me and him when Dad stiffened and sent me a stare that would kill other people. Dad had never touched me, aside from fixing my hockey hold or straightening my back, but his expression was murderous, and that meant the curses would fly, and he'd take out his impotent rage on me with words. He leaned over the barrier and my heart skipped; my chest tightened. I held my position and tilted my chin as he lowered his voice, hate dripping from every word.

"I warned you, Shaun." He stopped and let the words hang ominously until all the fight in me was gone. Only when I was quiet did he continue. "You know that kid's not right. He's like a freaking girl, and hell, if you get mixed up with him again…" he snorted. "Do you want people to think you're queer?"

I wanted to fight back, to stand up for what I believed in. I wasn't a kid. I was almost an adult now, but fear of losing my dad's approval, of messing everything up, of him finding out about *me*, kept me silent. So, I nodded, feigning compliance, while inside, I was a mess.

Kenji had been my closest friend. We'd understood each other and when he'd come out to me I'd helped him, listened to him.

If only we were still friends maybe I could have had someone to talk to.

"Jeez, Dad—"

"If you want to get to the NHL, then you don't let his kind of queer poison in your life. I've told you to stay away from him, and you were a good kid and did as you were told. Don't fuck it up now he's landed back in your goddamn school."

I'd been thirteen when dad had told me what I needed to do to get to the NHL, the big time, a chance to play with some of the best, to showcase my skills. Stay away from the queer kid. Throw away friendship. Work harder. Do better. The NHL was all I'd dreamed about.

All that Dad *ever dreamed about.*

"Dad—"

"Stay away from that kid," he warned.

I opened my mouth to respond, but he snarled at me, daring me to fight back, and somehow, I stopped talking.

Stopped thinking for myself because it was safer that way.

Worked the exercises and attempted to ignore Kenji.

But, wishing I could say hi and we'd go back to being friends again. Did he want to be my friend after I'd cut him out of my life, ignored his messages, pretended he didn't exist?

My dad's words, the fear in Kenji's expression, and I'd backed down. What thirteen-year-old kid doesn't want to make their dad proud?

He'll ruin everything for us.

What thirteen-year-old kid could fight back?

OVER THE NEXT FEW WEEKS, MY EARLY MORNING practice space became *ours*. Mine and Kenji's. Me at one end with my cones and the net, him at the other, with his twirls and jumps and dance moves that filled me with awe.

The entire school had become *ours*. We even had a couple of classes together, but we did a very good job of ignoring each other, or he ignored me and, well… I feared what he'd say to me if I tried to start a conversation. Sometimes, I would feel the weight of his stare, but we weren't friends, and when I caught his gaze, he'd turn away fast, but not before I'd seen a world of anger and hurt in his eyes.

I glanced across the ice, my gaze drawn to him standing on the other side deep in conversation with Ilya, his coach, and all around as big a controlling asshole as my dad. I didn't like Ilya.

I didn't like how he was with Kenji. Always

shouting, berating Kenji for not being good enough, fast enough, or strong enough.

I tore my gaze away from Ilya's latest criticisms after Kenji came out of a spin and fell, focusing instead on the task at hand. Coach Sennett was waiting for me, his clipboard in hand and determination on his face. I made my way over to him, trying to shake off the butterflies that had settled in the pit of my stomach. I needed to focus on hockey, not try to listen to the exact words Ilya was using with Kenji. I heard slurs about Kenji's weight; I saw Kenji slump out of the corner of my eye; I wanted to know what was going on, but like every other morning, I did nothing, because Kenji didn't want to even look at me, let alone talk to me.

"Morning, Coach," I greeted him, forcing a smile that felt more like a grimace. "You're here early."

"Morning, Shaun," he replied, his voice brisk. "Ed."

He acknowledged my dad, but they would never be friends. Particularly given how much my dad kept saying I was too good for the school team, and how much he wished I'd move to the Crestwood Sports Academy, a specialized academy outside Toronto. I wished I could care about Dad and Coach hating each other, but I was used to it by now—I just hoped

Coach didn't think I felt the same way. A team was only as good as its weakest player, and I was a good captain who cared.

"You ready for tonight's game against the Sunbury Cats, Shaun?"

"Of course he is," Dad said, with a sneer. Sometimes, I wished he wouldn't be such an asshole, staring down at people and judging them.

I nodded, my mind on Kenji. "I've been practicing hard."

Coach Smith studied me for a moment, his eyes narrowing. "Good," he said finally, his tone clipped. "But this team isn't just on you." My dad inhaled, but then the coach glanced at his watch. "Practice is done," he announced, and they headed into an epic staring match before Dad muttered something under his breath and stalked away.

"I meant we've all been practicing, Coach," I said, correcting myself as soon as Dad was out of hearing. No one else on the team was here at six a.m., every school day, and Saturdays, but that didn't mean the rest of the team weren't committed or didn't care. They just weren't obsessed like me.

Or obsessed like my dad.

"We need to win this game," Coach reminded me.

I nodded again, trying to push aside the sound of

shouting from Kenji's coach, and Kenji skating off the ice, his head high, but his brightness dimmed. "We won't let you down, Coach."

With those words hanging in the air between us, I turned away, my thoughts drifting back to Kenji, and headed to the locker room. We didn't often meet in there, he always left the ice first, but Ilya had kept Kenji back, the same leap and spin, over and over, until Kenji had to be dizzy from it. I kinda wanted to see him, maybe even talk to him, ask him to get together for a coffee or something? I didn't know, but Ilya had been shouting, and Kenji had fallen, and then, he'd been late off the ice.

There was no sign of him, and his bag wasn't still in his cubby—the one off to the left that he always used.

"Kenji?" I asked the empty room, but it was obvious he wasn't here, and something about that was wrong. I should've hurried in and spoken to him, asked him why Ilya was shouting. I headed into the bathroom to shower and heard sounds from a cubicle, the door half open, the sound of someone being sick and crying. Was that Kenji? Had he hurt himself in the fall?

"Kenji?" I asked, then pushed the door open and took in a hunched over Kenji with his fingers down his throat, tears streaming down his face. He stared up at me horrified and shoved past me, and I tried to catch him, stop him so I could ask about what I'd seen, but he was too fast.

And he ran.

Chapter Two

Kenji

Seriously, is there anything worse than the sound of a phone alarm beside your head at the ass crack of dawn?

The answer is no.

Rolling to my side, I swiped the stuff sitting atop my nightstand to the floor, where the phone landed, but continued to *beep-beep-beep-beep* and *buzz-buzz-buzz-buzz*. I knew what time it was without looking at my cell—five in the morning—the standard time for young men who trained under Ilya Sidirov to crawl out from under the covers where he was having a nice dream starring himself and Lenny Kravitz doing a pairs routine. Lenny was shirtless, which was not at all acceptable attire for a skater during a competition, but hey, if Lenny wanted to bare his chest, I wouldn't stop him. That man is delish.

The phone kept it up, vibrating under the bed on the hardwood floor.

"Ugh," I groaned at the incessant beeping and buzzing. Moving to my belly, I nudged Koro, my sobo's cat, who was nearly as old as my grandmother, but not nearly as nice. He hissed. I changed my mind and wiggled around the grumpy black cat with the ragged ear. He always slept with me. Not a clue why, as at any other time the ancient cat didn't like me much. Guess I had the best bed in the house. Sliding to the floor, the room dark, save for the light of the cellphone, I found where it had half slid underneath and now lay beside a pair of old hockey skates, way too small now, all covered with dust.

Good thing my mother didn't see the dust bunnies under my bed, or she would toss aside her paintbrushes and grab her Swiffer. Mom didn't like dust. Sobo liked it even less. Dad and I didn't care about dust. Which was obvious, given the thick layer coating all the junk under my bed. I grabbed my phone, silenced it, and then, caught by something like nostalgia, I pulled out the tiny black skates. Sitting on the floor in the dark in my sleep pants and a ratty T-shirt, I closed my eyes and let my fingers move over the laces. Memories of a childhood that felt as if it were ages ago, instead of just seven years, flowed over me. Ice hockey had been the sport that had gotten me onto the ice. I had always loved skating, so my father had signed me up when I was a kid.

Jun, my older brother, had no interest in sports of any kind. Much to the delight of Mom and Sobo, who were thrilled he was getting his masters in a field that would bring them honor. Mostly those were Sobo's words. She was old enough to still hang onto ancient ways of thinking. Mom was glad to have at least one child who wouldn't be hurt by strapping on blades. Dad, ex-flyboy in the US Air Force who'd turned to law enforcement after retiring and now worked in the state capital on the capital police force, loved having one boy who was as gung ho about athletics as he was. Imagine his shock when I announced, after playing hockey for several years, that I wanted to try figure skating.

Mom and Sobo had been thrilled. No one would punch me in the face repeatedly if I were figure skating. Jun didn't give a damn. He was too busy being the brains of the family, our own Asian-American Sheldon Cooper. So, I switched to skates with toe picks just as puberty was about to set in. Dad had commented once to Mom that he felt that this figure skating thing was a phase, and once I came out the other side of the hormone rush, I would see the light. He also had thought that my dating boys *and* girls was a phase at first. I've not grown out of figure skating or finding all kinds of people attractive.

Which went full circle to thoughts of Shaun Stanton. Shaun was my dream boy. Tall, strong, a jock. He and I had a history of sorts. We'd been the best of friends once, until his dad suggested hanging around with me was ruining his chances of being a hockey superstar. I'd wanted Shaun to tell him to fuck off. He didn't. I hated Shaun for it.

I think.

Only it was hard to avoid him now that we were at the same school.

A thud on the floor startled me from the past and Shaun's big blue eyes. Koro sat staring at me, cat-eyes glowing.

"Right, I know. You want treats."

He reached out to swat at me. Yep, treats. "On it," I said, stuffing the kiddy skates back under the bed, then getting to my feet. I yanked on some socks, then crept out of my room, past my parent's, and my grandmother's bedroom doors. I slid into the bathroom, used the toilet, washed my hands, and got on the scale. It read *121*, which meant I'd gained a pound since yesterday. Ilya would give me that *look* when he weighed me today. We did not skip weigh-ins. Fat skaters did not place in competition; he would tell me in that thick Russian accent of his.

I glanced at myself in the mirror to see if my face was puffier. No, I was okay. Five-foot-six and a hundred and twenty pounds was perfect according to my coach, so one-twenty it had to be. It could be water weight that had pushed me over. It could be that pizza I had chowed down on like a hungry dingo at dinner. Damn carbs. I knew better...

I flipped off the light, disgusted with my lack of discipline, and trudged downstairs to make myself breakfast.

Koro made his way down the stairs, his tail kinked at the top as he led me into the kitchen. He knew the routine in this house well.

I filled his bowl with dry food, which he ignored before opting to eat or starve. Not that the fat cat would wither away anytime soon. I flicked on the light, placed my phone on the counter next to the stove, and began whipping up some egg whites for a cheese and egg omelet while Dua Lipa sang about dancing the night away. I opted out of toast and sliced into a ripe avocado instead, shaking my butt to my favorite singer.

"No treats for you," I said to the cat, who was staring daggers at me. "Okay fine, I'll give you two."

I picked two tiny fish-shaped treats from the bag, then placed them on top of the dry food. The cat walked off. Cats. Oh. My. God.

I ate by myself, eager to get the food I wanted into me, instead of having to bicker with my mother and grandmother over eating a heartier meal. Sure, I loved my dad's American morning meals of pancakes and sausage. But I dared not let my weight get out of hand. If it did… well, then shit went sideways. So, counting calories it was. Lots of people did it every day. They had tons of apps for it. I used one. Not a biggie.

I wolfed down the omelet, then jogged upstairs to change into something casual to wear to the rink to skate for an hour or two before classes at Chesterford. Grabbing my car keys from my dresser, I shoved my wallet, books, and skates into my backpack. School was one of my escapes from skating if that made sense. Not that I didn't love skating. I did. But Ilya was intense. Like super intense as only an old-school Russian trainer could be. It was the ice or nothing. He disliked his skaters frittering away valuable training time with extracurriculars. You were either one hundred percent a figure skater—or you were not, he would say. And his methods paid off. I was doing well. Not as well as he felt I should, because no one ever pleased Ilya. And I would never tell him, but sometimes I wanted more from life than skating. Like maybe dating and dances and fooling around with friends at the ramen shop. Ilya had still not gotten over me disrespecting his wishes. He let me know that his students back in Belgorod would never have been so brash. I felt properly chastened but stuck to my guns like the typical American he often accused me of being. Yep, that was me, American as apple pie.

So yeah, I was super excited. I'd been homeschooled for a few years—it was simply easier to compete if we could work my schoolwork at our discretion—but coming into my junior year I had wanted more. I wanted to experience high school. I loved skating, and I wanted to continue, but I also maybe wanted to go to college. I went to dances, football games, and made friends. Like a normal teenager.

Well, mostly normal, if normal meant driving to the school rink before the sun was up to train. Which meant I was not normal at all, as every other student was still in bed right now. Almost every other student. There would be one other person there.

Shaun Stanton.

He was the only one I knew of who put as much into his sport as I did. Birds of a feather, we were once called, back in the day when we were playing hockey on the same team. That was before things had gotten weird. Before I'd left hockey for figure skating. Before I'd been talked into homeschooling by Ilya.

Parking behind Shaun's blue truck, I turned off my sporty little VW Jetta, the tunes dying away as the engine *tick-tick-ticked*. I stared hard at the bumper of the azure Ford pickup, my sight locking on the *GO COYOTES* bumper sticker plastered next to a Chesterford parking permit sticker like mine. My bumper had a pink, yellow, and cyan pan heart sticker next to the permit, just to let the world know who I was. My dad had bought it for me at Harrisburg Pride last year. He'd learned a lot about queer kids in the past few years, and now marched with me, Mom, and Jun every June for Pride. Sobo was too old to march, but she wore a rainbow wig to show her support of her youngest grandson. A big step away from her very traditional Japanese upbringing.

Shaun's truck kind of intimidated me. No, that

was a lie. The feelings I had for Shaun and about Shaun were what always had me sitting here working up the courage to go skate. We rarely spoke other than a perfunctory "*Yo*" to each other as we did our thing. Him shooting pucks or working on stick handling on one end of the ice, while I twirled, leaped, and snuck in quad jumps my coach admired, but the world skating organizations said I was too young to do as I was under nineteen. Silly rules.

Shaking off the funky vibes, I grabbed my bag and marched into the rink, giving the Coyotes banners, and snarling canine faces painted on the white walls a glance. I even patted the nose of the nearest coy-dog as I entered the rink, my bag bouncing off my backside as I jogged to the ice. Shaun was doing laps, his skates, and puffs of breath the only sound as he maneuvered the puck around small cones with incredible skill. I'd never had those kinds of hands when I played. I was more a speedster, taking the puck down the ice at Mach speed, then getting knocked off the puck by a much larger player. I'd never been beefy. Shaun glanced my way as I sat on the home bench, my hair pulled back out of my face with a bright yellow hairband.

My skates were black, like his, but smaller and narrower with the toe picks all the hockey players teased us figure skaters about. I tied my skates, shucked off my jacket, and stepped out onto the ice. *My* end of the ice.

Whenever I saw him, I had a flashback to when Shaun had walked in on me, pushing into my life uninvited as always, and had seen me trying to purge. Or had he? The expression of horror on his face that day said yes, he had witnessed me trying to get rid of the anxiety balled in my gut like castoff fishing line along the shore. My insides always felt tight, cutting off my ability to digest and to breathe at times.

He'd never said a word to me about what he had or hadn't seen. Then again, he'd not said much to me at all after that day. Our friendship had died a slow death. Much like an orchid left to wither in a dark corner with no water or sun. Now, here we both were, at the same school, sharing the same ice, and still not speaking. Some days, I wanted to march up to him and demand he speak to me. Tell me what he'd seen. Explain that I'd done that once. Clarify I'd spoken to a counselor a few times, and I was now eating as I should to maintain weight.

Maybe I should just skate up to him. Get in his face. Ask him why he'd dumped me like a used tissue. I paused in my warmup and waved a few fingers, the lights of the rink picking up the sparkly nail polish I'd put on last night. His blue eyes widened. Such pretty eyes. He ducked his head. Was that shame or shyness? When he glanced back, he looked as if he were going to say something more than that stupid broski *yo* I always got. My heart sped up a tick. What would I say if he moved to my end of the ice? Would I shout at him or offer him a kind word? I had no clue. As it turned out, what might have happened, never took place because his father arrived. Mr. Stanton was beyond driven. I had never cared much for Shaun's father. Shaun tore his gaze from mine and went back to hockey.

Whatever. Probably that was for the best. Shaun didn't need to be spending his ice time talking to someone as undisciplined as me.

We returned to our little worlds. Mr. Stanton shouting at Shaun. Ilya barking at me. For an hour, we did our work, then, at the end, when both adults had left the ice, I was wiping the sweat from my neck when a puck slid to a stop in front of me. I glanced over about ten feet, and there stood Shaun, also soaked with perspiration, hockey stick in hand.

"Hey," he said, and I swear if he hadn't been in skates, he would have been scuffing his feet. "Can we talk?"

I lowered my towel, the pull to say something to

him so strong I wet my lips to speak. Then, I remembered he'd been the one to ghost me.

I kicked the puck back to him, then skated off, tears welling as I headed to the locker room.

I left him standing.

Chapter Three

Shaun

I watched Kenji leave, frustrated he wouldn't stay and that I hadn't managed to speak. Why did I even ask if I could talk to him? I should've just blurted everything out.

Kenji, I'm bi.

    Kenji, I'm hiding.

    Kenji, I really hate your coach.

    Kenji, did I really see you make yourself sick? Are you okay?

    Kenji, can I look after you?

    Kenji, please can we talk?

· · ·

"Eyes front," Dad muttered behind me.

I had to force myself away from staring at the door Kenji had passed through, and back to Coach, who was heading this way along with another man, who extended his hand.

"Shaun Stanton? My name is Leo Bryant, and I work with Edge Sports Management."

"For real?" I said, flustered, as I shook his hand.

"For real," Leo smiled.

"Sorry, I'm just… Tennant Rowe is one of my favorite players, and his son, Soren is here, on the team, I mean, and…"

"Take a breath, kid," Coach Sennett said with a laugh.

"Sorry, yes, I'm Shaun."

"Coach Sennett here asked me to come watch you play."

"He did?" I glanced at Coach, who offered me a smile, then scowled at my dad, who'd crowded me and extended a hand to shake the agent's as well.

"Ed Stanton," dad began, "I've had professional playing experience."

Leo didn't seem to recognize him, which I bet dad hated. Still, they shook hands, but Leo soon focused back on me. "Have fun tonight," he said, and then, Coach Sennett urged him away and over to the seating where the two men laughed and did this whole bro-hug thing.

"This is it, son," Dad said and thumped my arm. "Finally."

"I've had scouts watch me before." Why did I sound so dead? Where was my enthusiasm? Why could I only think about Kenji and the way he'd stared at me as if I'd broken his heart?

"Yeah, but *his* agency reps some of the big guys, okay? You'd better play the best you can tonight, kid."

"Sure, Dad." Again, where was the life? Why did I feel so...

... wrong?

"I mean it, kid, don't fuck this up for us."

"Okay."

What else could I say?

THE REST OF THE TEAM WERE CONGREGATING BY THE door onto the ice, waiting for their captain. I headed over, removed my guards, and then, everyone gathered around me, and I tapped the floor with my stick.

"Okay, we know these guys. Soren, eyes on number ten, okay?"

"Yes, Cap."

"Don, Felix, keep it tight in special teams. Tyler, you're small and fast, and they hate you buzzing around, so stay on net, okay?"

"Yes, Cap," they chorused.

"Coyotes on three." We all reached into the middle of our loose huddle, touching hands, and then, as one, we all shouted "Coyotes!" before taking the ice. I skated a lazy circle at our end, watching the Sunbury Cats down at the other end. The Cats were a formidable team—an opponent we matched—and the excitement of the game curled in my belly. I caught a flash of pink in the crowd, and though I knew it couldn't be Kenji—he never watched our games—my heart skipped until I saw a mom with a bright pink bobble hat. Not Kenji.

The disappointment followed me into the first period, and somehow, by the end of it, my lackluster performance and disconnected thoughts meant the Coyotes were two goals down.

We only just scraped those two back in the second

period, and if we didn't pull ourselves together, we were going to lose this.

Wait. If *I* didn't pull myself together.

I paced the locker room in the second break, not quite connecting with the team, knowing in my heart that Leo out there seeing me at my worst, but not finding it in myself to care.

All I could think about were dark brown eyes and pink hair, and the hurt in Kenji's eyes. Fuck!

"Okay," I said and stopped pacing, all eyes were on me, even Coach, who'd stayed quiet this break so far. "Sorry," I added, and there was murmuring.

"Sorry for what, Cap?" Soren asked, his frown deep.

"For me, for this, for… let's get back out there and take this back. You with me?"

The team gathered around in that loose circle again.

"Coyotes!"

I could feel the weight of the team's expectations resting on my shoulders as the captain, and the agent who could be assessing me, a bemused coach, and my dad at the glass trying to catch my eye so he could tell me to stop fucking up. The Cats weren't interested in letting us pass, and we were two minutes out from the end before we gained proper control.

Soren zipped across the ice, scanning for an opening. I saw him make eye contact with Don, who was hovering near the blue line, ready for the pass. Soren flicked the puck towards him, and Don caught it on his stick. Without hesitation, Don sent a crisp pass my way, and I was right there, ready to receive it.

It glided towards me, and the pressure built because I had to make this shot count. With a quick flick of my wrist, I maneuvered it past the opposing defenseman and onto my stick. I could see the Cats' goalie, Evan, eyeing me warily from his position in the crease. He was good, but I knew I could beat him.

I skated closer to the net, the crowd noise deafening. I could feel my heart pounding as I lined up the shot and Evan shifted a little, trying to anticipate any move I could make, but with a swift motion, I released the puck, sending it soaring towards the top corner of the net.

Time seemed to slow as I watched the puck sail through the air. It was a perfect shot, and I could see the horror on Evan's face as it whizzed past him and into the back of the net. The crowd erupted into cheers, and my teammates rushed to congratulate me as I skated back to the bench.

With only a minute left on the clock, the

momentum shifted in our favor. The Cats' defense was rattled, and we took advantage of their disorganization to score another goal in the final moments. When the buzzer sounded and we'd won, the sense of triumph and relief was overwhelming.

As we skated off the ice, I couldn't help but feel a surge of pride in the team. Somehow, they'd worked around my lack of attention and kept us in the game, and it was moments like those that reminded me why I loved this game, and why I was proud to be their captain.

I skated over to the bench, still buzzing from the adrenaline of the game, but my excitement faded quickly as I saw my dad waiting for me, arms crossed and a scowl on his face. I sighed inwardly, bracing myself for the criticisms I knew were coming. It wasn't that I didn't value his opinion, but sometimes it felt like he was more focused on pointing out my mistakes than celebrating the wins, and I was growing tired of everything.

"You were sloppy out there, Shaun," he started, not even waiting for me to sit down. "You missed that pass in the second period, and your positioning on defense was terrible."

"Yeah, I know, Dad," I reply, trying to keep my tone neutral. "I'll work on it for next time."

Before my dad could launch into another round of critiques, Coach Sennett approached, followed closely by Leo, who smiled.

"Nice recovery," he said and patted my arm.

"The team let him down," Dad snapped.

I stiffened. I knew he'd be like this, but I had to ignore the tension radiating from my dad. "I let the team down," I blurted, and my dad went scarlet. "I got in my head, and it was bad."

"That Soren kid, just because his dad plays for—"

"I like that you saw that in yourself and recovered," Leo interjected and left my dad blustering. "Not everyone your age would be that self-aware. I was impressed by your performance out there today. Have you ever considered playing college hockey?"

My dad jumped in before I could respond. "Actually, we've been looking into Crestwood Sports Academy outside Toronto with a view to QMJHL. Shaun's goal is to go straight to the NHL."

Leo met my dad's gaze, not backing down. "I understand *your* aims, Mr. Stanton, but I was speaking to Shaun," he said. "I'd like to hear his thoughts on the matter, given he'd probably have his pick of scholarships should he choose the college route."

I shifted uncomfortably, caught in the middle of their exchange. On one hand, I owed Dad, and I always wanted the NHL—it was our shared ambition.

I think.

I knew that college hockey could be a valuable opportunity, and if there was a scholarship, then...

"I... uh... what Dad said... but... maybe," I stammered, feeling the weight of their expectations bearing down on me.

Leo nodded, and it seemed he was satisfied with my half response, although my dad's gaze was boring holes in me. "That's understandable. Take your time to consider your options." He handed me a card, which Dad took from me, so Leo, with exaggerated patience, handed me another one. "You understand, if you decide on an agent at this stage, then you're ineligible to go the college hockey route."

"I do."

"Okay, then call me if you'd like to talk informally about your options, about what we can do for you to support you in whatever you choose."

"Not without an adult present," Dad snapped.

Leo inclined his head. "Of course."

"No one decides anything for Shaun, but me."

Leo's eyes widened a little. "I'm sure what you're

saying is that Shaun gets to decide his path in life. Right?"

"With my guidance," Dad sneered, going on the defensive.

Great way to rile up my dad, who'd gone from smiling to temper in an instant—and so Leo would become yet another person my dad was going to rail against.

I glanced at Coach Sennett, who gave me an encouraging nod. Suddenly, the prospect of college hockey seemed a valid one, even if my dad was near imploding next to me, and even though it went against everything I'd worked for.

"Thanks, Mr. Bryant," I said, trying to muster up some genuine enthusiasm in the face of my dad's anger. "I'll definitely keep it in mind."

Leo extended a hand, and we shook. "Keep the card, and call me Leo, okay?"

As Leo and Coach Sennett moved off to talk to some of the other players, my dad turned to me, his expression unreadable.

"College hockey, huh?" he said, his tone laced with skepticism and laughter. "What a freaking joke, and you realize that asshole agency supports those freaking queer players? What the fuck, Shaun, that's not proper hockey."

I shrugged, unsure of how to respond. I knew he was talking about Soren's dad and other players on the Railers, and others down in Boston. Deep down, I knew I needed to explore all my options, and part of me still wanted to believe I could make it straight to the NHL, and I knew that would keep Dad happy.

I owe him.

"Yeah, Dad," I replied. "It's just something to consider."

Or not.

Chapter Four

Kenji

ANOTHER DAY, ANOTHER MORNING ON THE ICE.
Another awkward hour spent pretending. It was
getting old.

It was stupid. We'd been so close. As I watched
him from the bench—my practice bag beside me—an
old memory bubbled up. The first time Shaun had
eaten at our house when we'd been kids. Maybe
eight? He'd been so shy. Mom had to prompt him to
remove his shoes at the door. Shaun was beet-red as
Sobo explained that no one in our culture wore shoes
inside. He'd taken the slippers my father had offered
him, still glowing bright cherry, and removed his
scuffed sneakers. His big toe stuck out of his left

sock. I ran off to get him a pair of my socks to put on, and he had thanked me so many times that I had to give him a noogie to get him to stop. Then, there was the meal itself, where he'd had his first experience with chopsticks. Jun, my older brother, had ended up going to get him silverware to use. He couldn't get a noodle to his mouth, and we didn't want him to go hungry. He would have too because he would have sat there until he mastered those chopsticks. That was Shaun.

"Yo," he called across the ice, his expression hard to read as he returned to guiding the puck around the cones.

"Yeah, yo," I sighed as I toed off my sneakers, and put on my skates, lacing them, and taking the time to think about what to say next.

I stood there for a few seconds, arms crossed, watching Shaun working that lost puppy look to perfection, when I realized I was done with this. This weird state we were now in was not cool. Not at all.

"Hey, Shaun, you like Dua Lipa's music?" I called. His gaze lifted from the puck, his brows beetling as he stared at me as if I'd asked him if he liked pickled plums. I did, but that was neither here nor there.

"Uhm, sure. She's hot."

I rolled my eyes and skated over at a slow pace as he watched me coming closer. "I didn't ask if you would smash her, you thirsty dog. I asked if you liked her music. Do you? Like her music? You used to be into K-Pop back in the day."

He ran a hand through his sweaty hair, his expression shifting impossibly fast. "I… well you kind of played nothing but BTS, so I kind of picked it up."

"Hashtag Jimin forever." I smiled, then threw up two fingers crossing two fingers to make a hashtag. I knew I was acting like a tool, but we hadn't shared this many words since I'd arrived at Chesterford last fall. "So, do you like her music?"

"Sure," he replied, resting his stick on his wide shoulders, his hands gripping each end. It was such a hockey player stance that I had to chuckle. "What?"

"Oh, nothing." I waved my giggles off. "Would you mind if I played some of her music while I skate? I'm working on a routine that I want to perfect, then show to Ilya for a possible upcoming competition."

He frowned at the mention of my trainer who'd left the rink to answer a call. Then he cast a glance over his shoulder at the place his dad usually stood. There was no sign of him either, and for once the two of us were actually alone.

"What was that look for?"

"I… nothing."

"Look, if I said something—"

"I need to practice and so do you."

I spun from him, pulled out my phone to cue up my music, and tucked it into the band on my arm. Headphones and earbuds were not allowed on most ice rinks, so this set-up worked for me. Shaun stood at center ice like a dork. I ignored him, putting my mind to the task of perfecting my triple lutz, triple loop. It was an awkward transition in the program for me for some reason, and while I could usually nail it, the past few days I'd been under-rotating and getting shit from Ilya. So, I cued up the music Ilya had chosen for me, boring AF classical stuff, and moved into my warmup routine. I was too upset to focus on Dua. Throughout the warmup, there stood Shaun, watching, making me nervous with his big blue eyeballs glued to my ass.

After two failed attempts to land my jumps, I spit out a few choice curses in Japanese that my grandmother was known to say and skated over to the moose at center ice.

"What?!" I shouted over the harpsichord or whatever it was blaring out of my cell.

"I don't understand. You met Trent Hanson!" he yelled.

I stared up at him in confusion before reaching up to pause my music. "And?"

"And I thought you might switch trainers after meeting with Trent."

"Why would I do that? I meet lots of trainers and choreographers, and don't jump ship to sign on with them."

His nose crinkled in frustration.

"You should get away from Ilya. He's not good for you. His methods are primitive, he's a bully, and his effect on your mental health is—"

A queasiness blossomed in my belly. He was serious. How *dare* he hit me with that bullshit? He did *not* just say all that to me.

"Are you shitting me with this right now?" I snapped. He stood his ground even though I was about to jab him in his stupidly wide chest. "I mean pot kettle, Stanton! Do you even see what your father does to you on a daily basis?!"

"What? Of course… my dad isn't a problem."

"Oh really? Man, you are so dense. Did you take a puck to the skull recently? Your father is the fucking king of bullies. The king!" I jabbed him even though I knew he wouldn't feel it with the padding under his sweater.

"My father is driven to see me succeed. He's not

telling me that I'm fat all the time. Kenji, I know you have trouble with—"

"No! No, you do *not* get to talk to me about anything like that! You gave up all rights to talk about personal stuff with me when you threw me away like a rotten banana peel."

"I didn't…" He ran a big hand down his face. "Look, I don't want to fight with you, but I'm worried. You should look into signing with Trent."

"Okay, well, first thing, Trent isn't a trainer for skaters at my level that I'm aware of, but even if he was, I've done well with Ilya." He gaped at me. "Yeah, so there is that, and then, there is this. Stop talking about shit that you know nothing about!"

"It's just that—"

"No! I'm placing well in all my competitions, thanks very much. Also, who I train with is really none of your business. Is it?" I poked him in the chest with a thin finger, yet again.

"No, I guess not. But Trent wouldn't be making you—"

And he skidded to a halt, his words ending as if he had skated off a cliff.

"What? Trent wouldn't make me do what?" I demanded.

"Nothing. Nothing. Ilya is fucking god come down to bless you with his mad skills."

I blinked. What the hell was his deal? "Ilya is one of the best. He left Russia to—"

"Does he weigh you every day?" Shaun blurted. "Why does he do that? It's wrong?"

"I…" I choked up. "You don't get to make calls about my body!" I snarled low just in case anyone was listening.

"But Ilya does?"

I hated this so much. I'd thought, perhaps, he had forgotten. But no, of course not. Shaun Stanton had a slapshot that could rival Tennant Rowe's and a memory like a steel fucking trap. He had cut me out of his life. He'd stopped being my friend, but he still seemed to think he could get away with telling me what he thought.

"You have no clue," I whispered, then spun away, anger making me see red.

"Shaun!" his dad called him, all irritable and red in the face. But Shaun ignored him.

"I know what I know, Kenji," he said. "I saw—"

I spun, ice chewing under my skates, to glower at him. "You saw *nothing*. I have things under control. Everything is under control. So why don't you just mind your own fucking business and stop preaching at me like you care."

I stormed off the ice, right to the locker room, not caring if Ilya came back from his call and I was missing. Instead, I threw myself around like a dervish, cursing and crying until I shut myself in the bathroom and collapsed to the floor in a heap of trembling legs that wouldn't support me in a simple spin, let alone a quadruple lutz.

Chapter Five

Shaun

I WATCHED KENJI LEAVE AND WAS TORN BETWEEN following him or giving him space.

He wasn't wrong about Dad, but his words stung like a slap to the face, and I'd wanted so much to hug him close and tell him that worrying about him was my business because I cared. But I couldn't tell him that. Not now. Not in this world where being thoughtful was some marker that made me wrong, and different, and not the kind of mean-ass hockey player everyone wanted me to be. I hated to think what would happen if I showed vulnerability to anyone, or if a stranger saw me hugging Kenji, or heard me telling the vibrant kid who'd cut himself off from me that I understood some of what he felt?

I didn't have the right to criticize Kenji at all.

But I cared about him, however much people told me I shouldn't, and ever since… when I'd found him making himself sick…

I cared about him.

"Shaun! Move yourself!" Dad shouted.

I ignored dad. Thinking about when Kenji's dark eyes had met mine at first, and for a moment, I thought we could talk, and I swear I saw a flicker of the friend I once knew. But any connection had been quickly replaced by a guarded expression, and then, the anger, and me saying things I shouldn't have.

Why did I bring up what I saw?

Why mention it?

The need to protect him, to make him see it was all wrong and hold him close, was a dangerous thought, but I couldn't deny all the emotions making me burn inside, and I couldn't stand by and watch him suffer in silence. I was angry with him for shutting me out, and frustrated at my stupidity, but I owed it to him and our shared history to at least try. Maybe, just maybe, I could reach out to him, without exposing my secret to him or to anyone else. Kenji deserved better than the isolation he seemed to be drowning in, and I couldn't let my default to fighting get in the way.

"Jesus, Shaun! Pay attention!" Dad shouted. His harsh tone cut through my thoughts like a knife, snapping me back to the present and away from standing like an idiot staring at a closed door. Great, I'd stood still for too long, and now I was tense, could feel the stiffness in muscles that had cooled during my moment of distraction. Dad was going to be pissed—more pissed than he was now—and that was the last thing I needed today.

I took a deep breath and attempted to shake off the cold that had settled over me. Losing that warmth in my muscles could mean trouble on the ice, and it took some time to ease into practice and regain any fluidity of movement. It was like trying to thaw frozen gears and get them running again, and god, did Dad know that I'd fucked up. Case in point, his running commentary.

You lack determination.

You're weak.

Push harder.

At least, he hadn't pulled out his usual comment on how much he'd sacrificed. Still, I owed Dad for the early mornings, driving me everywhere, the equipment, and the time he gave up to work with the school team. Forget about Kenji. Focus on myself.

I clenched my fists inside my gloves, determined to prove to Dad, and myself, that I was trying, and that it didn't matter how much I wished I could hug Kenji and be there for him. Finally, I could think of nothing but my skates, and the ice, and hitting pucks from angles other NHL wannabes would never try.

Which is *exactly* how things should've been.

PHYSICS WAS ONE OF MY FAVORITE CLASSES. NOT only was it a subject that had always intrigued me, but Mrs. Anderson, our teacher—a middle-aged woman with corkscrew curls and a loud laugh—had a perpetual air of excitement about her subject and a way of explaining complex concepts that made them almost seem simple.

I loved this class.

So why was I staring out of the window? Why couldn't I get my head into the lesson when I knew damn well that the next time we were in this class there was bound to be a pop quiz.

Why couldn't I get Kenji out of my head?

The topic of the day was Newton's laws of

motion, and Mrs. Anderson was describing the third law to the class.

"Shaun Stanton!" someone called, and I snapped back into the room. "And the third law is?"

Shit. It was something to do with object A pushes or pulls on Object B with a certain force, and blah blah. What in Hell's name was wrong with my head?

"Sorry, Mrs. Anderson," I apologized, as she peered at me over the top of her scarlet glasses and sent me a look; the one that made me feel like an idiot.

Which I was.

Because my rambling thoughts about how I'd messed up with Kenji, and hockey, and my future didn't belong in the classroom.

"Pay attention, Shaun. Can anyone else... Felix Sinclair?"

I glanced at my fellow hockey player, who cocky as hell, laid out the entire third law from memory, then smirked at me. Ass. A good friend now that he'd gotten his head straight and fallen for Soren—a talented skater, but an ass.

"Very good, Felix. So, when..."

My mind drifted again, and my fingers found the edge of my notebook. I started scribbling in it, creating spirals, jumps, and lines that seemed to take on a life of their own. In my imagination, those lines were all about the third law, pushing off and stopping, turning into the graceful movements of skates on ice, gliding effortlessly across a frozen rink. It was a world away from the physics equations on the whiteboard.

Suddenly, Mrs. Anderson's voice broke through my reverie. "Shaun!" I sat up straight. "Care to share what's so fascinating in your notebook?"

My face was red with embarrassment. "Sorry, Mrs. Anderson. I was distracted."

The class snickered. Felix and Soren loudest of all.

Mrs. Anderson crossed her arms over her chest, and I swear she tapped her foot. "An essay on the third law, on my desk by Friday, two thousand words, and try to stay with us for the remainder of the lesson."

Shit. This was what I got for losing focus, essays on top of coursework and everyone chuckling at my misfortune. I nodded, feeling sheepish, and forced myself to focus on the lesson once more, closing my notebook with determination, only to open it again when I realized I should take notes. When the class ended, I gathered my things and scurried out of the classroom—eager to escape the embarrassment of being called out and the chance of Mrs. A catching me—darting away from other students piling out of rooms and hurrying around the corner.

And collided with someone smaller, lighter, and way too easy to knock over. It was like crashing into a fragile vase amidst a sea of sturdy books, and boy were those books flying.

Kenji. Sprawled on the floor, his expressive dark eyes wide as he gazed up at me with a mix of surprise and shock. He looked so little down there, fragile almost, tiny in his school uniform, and my heart raced as I extended a hand to help him up.

"Kenji, shit. I'm sorry," I stammered, feeling a rush of guilt for sending him tumbling. "Are you okay? Did I hurt you?" I had to have hurt him. I was a foot taller, and god knows how many pounds heavier.

He accepted my hand, allowing me to pull him to his feet, and straightened his clothes with a nonchalant air as sniggering kids walked past, taking pleasure in someone else's embarrassment. I sent them the hardest glare I knew, but clearly I wasn't doing my best at being intimidating when they kept grinning. Kenji's initial surprise soon gave way to anger. He stared up at me with narrowed eyes, his lips pressed into a thin line, frustration in his posture, his body tense and his shoulders squared.

Kenji's voice carried a sharp edge as he confronted me, his annoyance clear. "Shaun, the fu— seriously? Did you even look where you were going?"

I blinked, taken aback by the question. It was a valid inquiry, considering it was my lack of attention that had led to our collision, but I was lost for words as I checked Kenji for injury.

"I did… I was… sorry…" My irritation at being an idiot mixed with embarrassment. "I had a lot on my mind…"

"You freaking giant, people can get hurt!" Kenji's expression didn't soften as he picked up his books, Felix stopping by us to help him. I should help Kenji, but when I leaned down, he yanked the nearest book away from me.

He brushed himself off, and I watched him leave. I was the tallest and the biggest in this hallway, and somehow, I wanted to shrink into myself. I was a hockey player, I was built to be strong, and hip checking bigger men than me would all too soon be in a day's work.

Only Kenji was so small, so fragile… fuck… I *was* a freaking huge-ass immoveable monster.

"Kenji!" I called after him, but he raised a hand and gave me the finger.

"You okay?" Felix poked me in the belly, and I

was aware I hadn't moved from the spot where Kenji had bounced off me.

"Sure," I said, without meaning it at all. "You think he's okay?"

People began to slope away to the next class, and I needed to move.

"Kenji?" Felix glanced at the corner around which Kenji had disappeared. "Yeah, sure." Although, he didn't sound convinced. "He's small, and you're…" He waved at me. "You."

"Exactly."

"He knows how to fall, Cap, he's had worse on the ice."

I followed Felix to the next class, ignoring his pointed glances until he stopped me with a hand on my arm.

"It's cool you wanna come with me, but I don't think you're in my Calc class."

Shit. What was wrong with me today?

"Heading that way." I gestured in the distance and carried on walking. I think Felix mumbled something like, "Sure, Cap."

And I was late to the next class when I had to double back after the coast was clear, which got another teacher glaring at me, and another class of kids chuckling at the big stupid hockey player.

Great.

"YOUR DAD'S ON A CALL WITH MR. BRYANT," MOM said the moment I walked through the door, barely having removed my coat and taking the time to hang it up and get my thoughts straight. This didn't bode well because Leo was, in his words, a sturdy wall that would stand between me and the rest of the world. Which, to my dad's dismay, meant getting between him and me. Leo wasn't pushing me to go into the draft when I was eligible or telling me I needed to go to college and work my way to the NHL that way. Dad had gotten over being pissed at Leo, over the moon that I'd finally done something right and snagged the attention of an agent from the team who worked with some of the guys on the Harrisburg Railers.

My dad's dreams had begun to come to fruition— as long as I did what Dad wanted and didn't listen to Leo at all.

Leo was more than just a guy who negotiated contracts and handled the business side of my potential hockey career, he was the person who was challenging me to think long and hard about what I wanted to do.

Take up the chance of attending a specialized boarding school, where hockey was everything, push hard for scouts and the NHL draft next year, and end schooling straight away.

Or stay here and wait another year.

Of course, Leo didn't know about me being bi. Hell, the only person that had any idea was Mom, and even then, it wasn't something we talked about. She just accepted me for who I was and worried every time my dad started using slurs about any hockey player not pulling their weight. My dad was intense. He had this idea of what a real man was, of what my career should look like, and he pushed, sometimes too hard, and occasionally I pushed back, but it was easier to back down. That was where Leo stepped in, a calm, steady force who told my dad what happened next, within reason, was my choice.

My career.

My life.

When Dad had spent our last meeting shouting his expectations and telling me I wasn't working hard enough, Leo was there to intercept, which I knew would cause me trouble after he left, but in the moment, it was everything. He had this way of handling Dad—firm, but respectful—making sure I could focus on the game and not get bogged down by pressure, but he also rode my dad to the point where his temper would snap and it would be me who endured that anger, even if Mom tried to get in the way.

"What are they saying?" I asked.

She tucked a stray blonde hair behind her ear and shook her head. "I don't want to listen…" She pressed a hand to her chest, and I winced. I knew how anxious she ended up when Dad was angry, and given the level of shouting, that was what was happening.

"Was Leo calling for me?"

"No, your dad called him…" She pushed\ a letter across the counter, and I didn't have to read it to know that it was another letter from Standings St John, detailing a scholarship as generous as it was short. The good players who ended up going there were the ones destined for draft, and most were in and out in two years, getting a place in the Junior Hockey League draft, then straight on to the NHL.

"The letter was addressed to me," I said, my tone dead.

"Your father doesn't mean to do the things he does."

I folded the letter and pushed it into my pocket. "Yes he does, Mom. He knows *exactly* what he's doing."

The office door slammed open, and Dad stormed out, Mom taking a few steps toward me, but I waved her back.

"Why did you open my mail?" I demanded as soon as I saw him.

Dad came right up into my space, his expression thunderous.

"You need to make a choice," he snapped at me. "You're fucking things up."

"I'm not going to Standings St John," I began, and he bristled.

"You're not old enough to get to decide for yourself!"

"I am, Dad." After a growth spurt over the summer, I was the same height as him now, six-foot, but broader and stronger, too, and I confronted him. My hands were shaking, fear rippling in me that I was even doing this, but I was done with today.

He snarled. "Who do you think you are—"

"And if you're not careful, when I turn eighteen, you won't have access to anything I achieve. No money."

"I don't want your money."

"Yeah, but what about no dad trips with my NHL team, no kudos from the media for being a great hockey dad. You want to lose that as well?"

He opened his mouth to say something. I expected his disapproval, and the hate-filled words he threw at me that he called encouragement, but muttering, he backed away.

"You could have been great," he snapped.

"I'm not leaving. Yet."

Because my mom would be on her own, with my dad, who thought the world owed him something, and because being up at dawn to the Chesterford ice, was my way of watching over Kenji.

I was determined that Mom would never know I stayed for her.

And as for Kenji—he didn't know it, probably wouldn't care if he did, and he hated me for what I'd seen.

None of that mattered.

I wanted to be the one who made everything right. I wasn't going anywhere.

Chapter Six

Kenji

ALEXANDER THE GREAT – A MIDTERM ESSAY BY KENJI Kelly

Before the days of drone strikes and computerized conference calls between the heads of state and the modern military, a lone man conquered one of the greatest empires of the known world with only his intelligence, his military genius, and a sword. His name was Alexander the Great, and his story is one of my favorite of all the historical figures that I've read about. Also, he was queer, and cool, and incredibly hot, with facial features like Shaun's and a build to match.

. . .

"WHAT THE FUCK?"

I stopped typing on my laptop to gawk at what I had written. Gods all be damned, as Dad liked to say when he thought Mom was out of earshot. This was what happened when you did your schoolwork at hockey practice. Your mind got muddied with watching the Coyotes captain and his team out there on the ice. I had an hour reserved for after the hockey team. Ilya would be here soon, and I would need to put my laptop away to focus on skating. And weigh in. I erased the bit about Shaun in my AP Histories of the Ancient Worlds class paper. I had three AP history classes under my belt, and this would be my fourth. That was how much I loved history. Can you say college-credited courses? Yep, I had three already. My secret goal was to become a history professor and try to instill a love of all things old to other kids who all seemed to hate history class and came crawling to me to help them with papers.

I glanced up after the Shaun bit was gone, my attention drawn to Soren and Felix standing in the corner having an intimate conversation. They weren't making out, but you could tell just by the way they looked at each other that they had something strong. I liked Soren and Felix a lot. They were kind of like relationship goal material. They'd started off bad but had somehow turned things around. I kind of wished I could figure out how to do that with Shaun.

But anytime we talked, he had to bring things back to the past. A place I did not want to revisit. I wasn't the same confused kid anymore. I was seventeen now and had a grip on things. Mostly. I guess I had as much of a grip as any other kid my age.

The coach whistled the guys in for a talk at center ice. I felt Ilya before I saw him. He simply had this presence. Mom liked to say that he blew into a room like a Siberian cold front, and that fit pretty damn well. He was cold, firm, and rarely smiled. Even when a student would place well and pull good scores, he would scowl, then point out where we could improve.

"Morning, Coach," I said as he sat down beside me cradling a takeout cup of black coffee. He was a stern man, in his late sixties, with a shock of silver hair and a trim mustache. Tall, thin as a pencil, he nodded in reply. Niceties and Ilya Sidirov did not chill together.

"They are late," he pointed out, jerking his hawkish nose in the direction of the hockey team. I nodded. They were. They knew it. It was a constant thing. "I will speak to them. You will meet me in the locker room for weigh-in, then we will work."

"Okay." He threw me a look. "Yes, Coach," I amended, shoved my laptop into my backpack, and took off for the locker room we shared with the Coyotes. I had one little cubby hole the team had graciously allotted me. Knowing that Ilya would be rousting the hockey team, I raced to undress, the chill of the rink settling over me as I waited in my underwear for my coach to return. He did, muttering in Russian, then led me to the weight room. I hustled along, my skin pimpled, as he droned on about disrespectful American ways.

I bobbed my head, rubbed my bare arms, and wished I had long johns on instead of dark green briefs.

"You will be fine. The cold is bracing. You would not have survived one winter in my village with your delicate ways," Ilya stated as I darted to the scale, then stepped on. Would it be better to hold my breath or release it. Did air weigh anything at all? Today was my solo day with Ilya. Group would be tomorrow morning at eight as it was a weekend. He had three other students, all girls, and they were as skittish about upsetting him as I was, maybe more so as they were known to leave the ice in tears. Not that I hadn't a time or two myself, but not as often. Ilya studied the digital readout, then sighed. "You are two pounds over. You must stop eating junk food. How do you plan to out skate your competitors at States when you are fat and flabby?"

"Sorry," I whispered, covering my belly with my cold hands. "I don't know why I'm gaining. I'm following the diet that I always have."

"Hanging out with your friends in the noodle shops, then eating potato chips at night. Lazy, slovenly habits that I feared you would acquire in this school." He waved a hand in the air. "I will note this down in my tablet. Tomorrow, I want to see improvement. Now, get dressed for the ice. We have much work to do on your routine before you are close to ready for the Eastern High School Regionals in March. Much work."

"Sorry, I'm sorry." I stepped off the scale just as the sound of twenty or so guys in skates passed by the open door. They all glanced in as they passed. Every. Single. One. Despite the cold, I was hot with embarrassment. Then Shaun walked by, sweaty and smiling, until he spied me standing there in my briefs, the scale behind me, Ilya at my side. The corners of his mouth fell from up to down in a microsecond. He took a step toward us. His coach appeared then, gave me and Ilya a look that was hard to discern, and led Shaun away by the elbow.

"Go, change. I will be on the ice." I nodded at Ilya, then scampered away, my feet chilled through my socks, into the locker room where everyone ignored me. What they were thinking I couldn't say, nor did I care. I was so ashamed of being seen in my underwear that I wanted to throw up. I swallowed down some bile as I dressed, pulling on some older black over-the-boot leggings and a sweater, and that was it.

I peeked up through my hair when skates appeared beside mine. My fingers stalled on the laces I was tying as I glanced up to find Shaun and his coach beside me. Coach Sennett was smiling down at me, Shaun's expression was neutral. My gaze darted around the locker room. To Felix, to Soren, to Tyler with his pink hair, and then, back to the two towering over me.

"Sorry we ran over," Coach Sennett said to me, his face a kind one. "Please tell Ilya that we'll be more attentive to the clock."

"I will," I replied, then worked up a wobbly smile of my own. "He can be a little…"

"Yes, he can be, but I understand," Coach said. "So, do you weigh-in every day for Ilya?"

"We do, yes." I got to my feet, grabbed my backpack, then shot Shaun a dark look because I just *knew* he was behind pulling his coach into my personal affairs. "There's nothing wrong with an athlete monitoring his weight and BMI, is there?"

"Nope, not at all. I just have to wonder if it's necessary to weigh in daily," Coach Sennett replied, his gaze filled with worry. Great. Now Shaun had his coach thinking stupid shit about my regimen. As if either of them knew what it took to be competitive in figure skating.

"Ilya thinks so, and since he won an Olympic medal—"

"Back when Khrushchev was the head of the Soviet Union," Shaun piped up, unable to keep his trap shut for five minutes. At least, he knew who Nikita Khrushchev was, fellow history nerd that he was. "No one does that anymore because it can lead to—"

"I have to get on the ice. My skate time is limited because the hockey team ran over."

With that, I stalked to the ice, leaving both of them—probably the entire Coyotes team—staring at my fat ass. UGH. *Why* was everyone so damned concerned with other people's business? I didn't tell them how to play hockey. I hit the ice with anger. It fueled me through a horrible session where I was on my ass more than I was on my skates.

"Enough!" Ilya shouted as I picked myself up after hosing up a simple salchow. "Where is your head today?! You are jumping into the ice instead of spinning off the ice. This is a jump I teach to six-year-olds. Get up. Go again. And if you do not land this, we are done for today."

"I'm not feeling well," I lied as I brushed ice off my sore backside. "I think I'm coming down with something." He eyed me with something akin to utter disappointment. "I feel sick."

That was no lie. My stomach was on fire, acid churning up into my throat.

"Go then. Go home to your mama and let her coddle you as if you were tiny baby. When you are ready to return to the ice as a man who can skate through a belly upset, then we maybe will continue. Perhaps by the time you are back from the diapers, I will have found a new skater who wishes to go to Michigan to be judged by the famed Petrova Kulikov."

"No, I… I'm okay. I just need to focus. It's easing up. The ice is choppy from the hockey team," I lied, swallowing hard as I shook off the failed salchow. "I want to go to Michigan, I do. I'll do better," I vowed to the man who stood at center ice, arms crossed, steely gaze pinned to me. "I'll do better."

"Go again," he ordered. I went again. And again. And again. When I got home after school, I took a hot bath, cried into the bubbles, and had a bowl of Sobo's Mentsuyu soup. No noodles, just the stock. Then, I went to bed, curled into a ball, and fell asleep in time to hear the beep-beep-beep and buzz-buzz-buzz as a new day dawned.

FRIDAY NIGHT WAS NOODLE NIGHT FOR THE HOCKEY team.

I knew this, as did the three girls who skated in group with me, which was the reason we were now at the Hot Pot Noodle Shop instead. I had no complaints about being the only dude at a table with three gorgeous girls. Anita, Evelyn, and Harper were tiny little things, like me, but even tinier. Thin as a whisper with big eyes and soft pink lips. They were juniors, as well, and quite popular. I sort of liked them sometimes, but they could be catty as hell. Like now, for example. They were gossiping about Tyler and Jonah behind their hands as if making fun of someone who wasn't rich was acceptable. Jonah came from a working-class family like I did, no shade from me about that at all. Sometimes, I wondered if the problem wasn't that Jonah wasn't wealthy, but that he was biracial. Like me. Saying they disliked him because of his skin tone wasn't acceptable, so they picked other reasons they felt were okay to run him down about.

When they started tearing apart his clothes, I got to my feet, my chair scraping over the floor of the eatery, pulling every eye in the place to me.

"You know clothes aren't really all that important," I snapped at the girls gaping at me as if I had gone over the edge.

"That's what we heard about you. Flashing your dick at the hockey team the other day," Anita the head harpy giggled. "We heard it wasn't much of a show."

The malice oozed off them. I was done with this shit. Stupid, petty high school bullshit. Like there weren't bigger issues in this world to worry about than someone's shoes. Honestly, sometimes going to a private academy was the shits.

I grabbed my coat and left, their titters following me out into the chilly late February night. I so needed to get into a club in school that had decent people. Maybe the history club. My AP history teacher, Mr. Amiti, led it, and he was cool. Fuck Ilya and his ban on anything other than skating after school. I needed more.

"Hey, Kenji.". I heard and rolled my eyes.

Shaun. I kept walking, my skates thudding into my back, my eyes on the prize—my VW parked a few hundred feet from the noodle shop. The wind was biting, making my eyes water as I surged forward. Shaun caught up with ease. His legs were much longer than mine. "Those skater friends of yours are hyenas."

That brought me to a halt, surprising him so bad he fumbled and fell off the curb into the side of a Buick. Thankfully, the alarm wasn't set.

"What the hell does that even mean?" I asked, wishing like hell he would leave me in peace. Why did he care so much? Why was he being so nice? I'd ghosted him years ago.

"It means they prowl around in a pack, cackling and snapping at everything and everyone," he answered, the cold wind playing with his hair. It looked soft.

I wanted to argue, but… yeah, that was a pretty good description of those three. "Okay, so they're hyenas, and you're a water buffalo."

His nose wrinkled in confusion. It was an expression I'd always found adorable.

"A water buffalo. How so, man?"

"Because you have a big head and like to run into people."

He barked out a laugh. I'd not heard him laugh in forever. "Shit, that is so stupid, yet amazingly precise. What are you, then?"

"I don't know. Something small that fucks up all the time. A dung beetle."

"Dude, dung beetles roll *the* tightest poop balls."

I snorted. "Tight poop balls. That'll be my claim to fame." I made an arc in the air with my hand. "Here lies Kenji Kelly, roller of immaculate shit balls."

"Epic epitaph."

"You're stupid." He chuckled, then nodded. "I'm sorry about those three. They're decent skaters, but they're so fucking snobby. I like Jonah, and Tyler, and all the guys on the team."

"Then why don't you come back inside and have some ramen with us?"

I stared back at the shop. My stomach snarled. I'd not eaten anything since lunch, and that was only half a turkey sandwich—no bread just the meat—and a pickle so I ensured I would make weight tomorrow morning. The neon lights in the windows of the Hot Pot called out like a siren to a lonely sailor out at sea.

"I should probably go home," I replied as I looked from the ramen shop window up at Shaun.

"You can go home later. It's only eight o'clock. I

know training is important, but so is being a kid, you know?"

I did know that. And I wanted it more than anything. I wanted to be a dumb kid with Shaun and the Coyotes. Shaun was giving me that stupid expectant golden retriever expression of his. My resolve weakened.

"I can't eat any of the deep-fried stuff," I answered. He smiled. "And no one mentions seeing me in my underwear."

A shadow moved over his face, then disappeared. "They won't say a word. I will grind anyone who makes fun of you into karashi."

"You included. Not a word about anything that has skates. Promise me."

He crossed his chest with his finger. "I promise. Come on. Have some soup, chill out. We can talk about that new Netflix documentary about Genghis Khan."

"Genghis Khan. Cool. Okay, history and soup, no skate talk, no deep-fried food."

"Yep." He," he nudged me with his shoulder, just enough to get my feet moving back in the direction of the ramen shop. "Nothing to make you mad. I promise."

I planned to hold him to that. "Did you know that

Genghis's father was poisoned by rival Tartars when he was only nine?"

"I think I read that somewhere."

The bells over the door of the noodle shop and the sounds of hungry, happy teenagers greeted us. Okay, yeah, this was maybe a good idea. Peeking at Shaun, grinning like he had won the lottery as he steered me past the trio of asps in Gucci to the Coyotes' table, made me feel a million and one things all at once. Every one of them tingly.

Chapter Seven

Shaun

As I led Kenji back to the table, relief washed over me like a warm wave. Seeing him settle into the seat next to Soren and Felix filled me with a mix of satisfaction and happiness. They'd shuffled along the bench to make room, offering fists to bump, all smiles, and I slid in beside Kenji, feeling a surge of elation that I'd convinced him to eat something.

I hunched over, so I wasn't looming as much, and watched everyone at the table when I couldn't shake the feeling of protectiveness that enveloped me as Kenji seemed small between me and Soren. I should have made it so he'd sat next to Tyler who was shorter and less threatening. My bad—I'd fix that next time.

Only, there was Tyler, across the table, his gaze settled on me with an unreadable expression, as if he didn't want Kenji at the table, which made no sense because Tyler was a good guy, and he and Kenji were friends. I kicked out to knock his foot and hit Dom instead, who'd been shoveling in an enormous amount of noodles.

"Watch it, Cap; I need my feet to skate," Dom grouched good-naturedly.

I winced. So much for tapping Tyler, who was still staring at me, making me uneasy, a knot of discomfort forming in the pit of my stomach. I wished I had gotten Kenji to sit next to Tyler instead, where I could keep an eye on him.

Felix leaned around Soren, nudging him out of the way, almost in Soren's lap.

"Hey, Kenji. Are you going to bust out the triple toe loop at the Snowflake Classic?"

Kenji paused, and then, it was as if someone had flipped his excitement switch. "Yeah, I've been practicing it a lot. I think I might just give it a shot," he replied. "That's if I get to go," Kenji murmured.

I hated that he sounded so flat. Of course, he'd go, I mean, I had no idea what the qualifications were for whatever the Snowflake Classic was, but Kenji was amazing, and he'd get a place.

"Do you have to earn a place?" Soren asked.

"Yes, and no. I mean, I've placed in all my events, but it's up to my coach if I'm ready." He pressed a hand to his stomach and bit his lower lip. "I want to go."

"What kind of sparkly stuff will you wear?" Dom asked.

I stiffened, waiting for the sneer, even though I knew Dominic Wishor was a good guy. He was big like me, rough around the edges, our biggest D-man, and had this way about him that was almost intimidating. In reality, he was a huge teddy bear who loved watching nature documentaries and cried at the last one he'd watched in my basement den because a couple of baby meerkats didn't survive an attack. "I saw your blue one, with the lines; it was cool."

"I have this black outfit, like an all in one, with a hood, and I added some diamonds to it, not real ones, of course." Kenji chuckled to himself. "But yeah, it's super pretty." Then, he stopped, as if he'd realized where he was—in the middle of a group of hockey players, and I swear, if anyone stepped out of line with him, I'd pummel them into the ground.

"So, when the light is following, you'll be all

shiny," Dom said. "I sure hope you go, and maybe we could all go up and watch? What do you think, Cap? Road trip?"

"We could get one of my dads to drive," Soren announced, "or Grandpa, if they're away."

Yes. Absolutely freaking yes. "Sure," I said instead, "sounds cool."

"You'd come?" Kenji asked, as if that were a brand-new concept.

Dom held out a fist to bump. "Team Ice," he announced, and Kenji reached out to touch his small hand to Dom's.

"Team Ice," he whispered.

"So, what kind of thing is a triple toe loop?" Dom asked eagerly, but again, Kenji was quiet.

"Yeah, what is one of those?" I asked lamely.

Kenji shot me a glance of irritation, the flash of it obvious in his gorgeous dark eyes. "It's kind of boring," he murmured.

Dom rested his chin on his hands and all I could focus on was the smear of sauce on his nose—I mean, who gets sauce on their nose? "I think it's beautiful," he said with a sigh. "If I hadn't got so big..." He rolled his eyes in self-deprecation, and I assumed he meant he might have turned his skating skills to the poetry of figure skating, rather than the brute force he showed in hockey.

Next to me, Kenji moved forward, resting his hands on the table. "Um, so the triple toe loop is one of those jumps where you really gotta nail the takeoff," he explained, and then, his hands were making shapes in front of him, and he wriggled against me as if his body recalled each movement. "You start with a strong edge, then you launch yourself into the air, pulling your knees tight to your chest to gain rotation. The key is to spot your landing and use your arms for balance as you come down." His voice was animated, and as Kenji demonstrated the triple toe loop with graceful gestures, he transitioned into another sequence. "And from there, you can flow right into a footwork sequence," he continued, as if the table was his rink, as if he were gliding across the imaginary ice. "You wanna keep the momentum going, linking one element to the next while maintaining speed and rhythm. It's all about showcasing your agility and musicality, while keeping the audience engaged." He finished his explanation.

Dom's mouth had fallen open. "Wow," he said.

I didn't like the *wow*. I didn't want to hear that wow. I was... I don't know... pissed at Dom.

"You have sauce on your nose," I pointed at Dom,

breaking the rapt attention of the people drawn in by the beauty of Kenji's words.

Dom scrubbed at his nose, and Felix took over the questions, which I tried to focus on given how much Tyler was glaring at me. I frowned at Tyler, asking him silently what was wrong. His gaze narrowed, and I thought he was angry at me. Not sure what for, but that was me. I wasn't good at picking up unspoken angst. Maybe, I'd done something, or said something, or maybe, and this was more likely, I'd pissed off his boyfriend Jonah, who was scribbling in a notebook. I didn't recall upsetting Jonah—he was the official team photographer, as well as all the other Chesterford teams, including I guess, Kenji. Whatever. I'd ask Tyler what the fuck he had going on with me after this.

Oh god, wait, did I have sauce on my nose?

I casually wiped it, just in case. But no, Tyler was still glaring.

"Anything else guys?" Tammy, our server, was scooting around picking up empty plates.

"What do you want, Kenji?"

"Oh, I haven't looked at the menu," Kenji spluttered.

I pointed at the wall opposite where the specific menu items were listed. "My treat," I added.

Kenji wriggled again, his hands clasped in his lap, biting his lip again. "Umm…"

"All the noodle options are good," I encouraged.

"I don't know…" Kenji murmured.

"Or rice, they have rice dishes." Kenji hunched in on himself, probably overwhelmed at the choices, and I patted his hand. "I can order for you," I said.

He stiffened and shrugged off my touch. "Vegetarian broth," he snapped at the server, or maybe at me, then softened the words with an apology to Tammy, who didn't seem fazed by any of it.

"You got it, sweetie, anyone else?"

The guys around the table put in orders, I added some of my favorite pickled radishes, a plate of vegetarian spring rolls—given I now knew Kenji liked vegetarian stuff—and another soda, and then, it was a waiting game for the food, and somehow no one was talking. Or at least, the ease of conversation about the figure skating had passed. Thankfully, the food began arriving, and I nudged the plate of spring rolls towards Kenji. "Here," I said, my voice soft. "You should eat something."

"No thank you," he said, and pushed the plate back to me, and I realized, of course, the damn things were fried.

"How about some radishes instead?" I offered him my bowl, but his glazed expression was a good enough answer, and then, his soup arrived. I mean, all the food in this place was good, but his soup was mainly some vegetables in a thin broth. No noodles, only a couple of mushrooms. Still, it was food, and he picked up the spoon and lifted a mouthful to his lips.

Someone kicked me under the table, and it snapped me out of the fact I was staring, and when I checked out who'd done it, Tyler was slumped in his chair, making cutting motions on his throat. They stopped when Kenji placed his spoon next to his bowl, so the indication that I needed to stop doing whatever I'd been doing was something Tyler didn't want Kenji to see. I was helping Kenji, just like I had wanted to. And what was wrong with that?

"So, how is the hockey going?" Kenji asked, nudging the bowl away, so animated that it was clearly an act.

"Good," Soren said. "We're…"

I let Soren explain because Kenji was leaving the soup.

He wasn't eating the damn soup.

Fuck.

Soren and Felix left then, plus Dom, and the other players down the table, until it was only me, Kenji,

Tyler, and a distracted Jonah, who was now fiddling with a camera.

"I need to go," Kenji murmured, his soup long since collected by Tammy, who never said a word that she was taking a near full bowl. "Can I get out?" He poked at me, and I slid out of the way, grabbing my jacket. "You don't need to leave on my account," he snapped, then sighed. "Sorry. Look, I need to go."

He sidestepped me and hurried to the door, letting in the cold before vanishing. I sketched a wave goodbye to Tyler, then headed out after him, catching him by his car. I wanted to ask him about why he hadn't eaten, and what was wrong, and why wouldn't his coach sign off for him to go that Snowflake thing, and why it was important for him to listen to me.

"You didn't eat!" I said instead.

He whirled on me. "You don't get to do that to me!" he shouted. "You made everyone watch me. You treated me like I was a kid! You made me feel sick!" He balled his hands into fists and pummeled my chest, and I let him. "I hate you!" Then, he climbed into his car before I could even think about what I'd done to upset him.

I watched the Volkswagen disappear around the corner and rubbed a hand on my chest. He hadn't hurt me, not really, but somehow, I'd messed everything up again.

"What the fuck was that?" Tyler snapped at me from behind.

"I don't know," I muttered as I turned to face him. "I don't know what's got into him."

"Not him!" Tyler was working his way up to angry, which took a lot. "You!"

He poked me in the chest at the same place Kenji had punched me, but this wasn't Kenji, and Tyler didn't get to poke me.

I brushed off his hand. "What?"

"You're such an idiot," Tyler muttered under his breath, his tone laced with frustration. "Why did you bring him in there, in front of all of us?"

"What do you mean? I was trying to be friendly, and we're not going to be nasty to him, so—"

"Stop!" Tyler sighed, running a hand through his pink hair. "Don't you see? Food is a battlefield for him. Forcing him to eat in front of others, especially when he's struggling, is just making things worse."

"I just wanted him to eat something."

"That's not how this works. Jesus!"

A hard knot formed in my stomach as Tyler's words sank in and guilt washed over me at the thought I'd unknowingly—stupidly—added to his distress.

"But I just wanted to help him," I protested weakly, feeling helpless in the face of Tyler's accusation.

"I know you did, Shaun," Tyler replied, his voice softening. "But sometimes, the best way to help someone is to give them space and support them from afar. Pushing them too hard can do more harm than good. Is he seeing a therapist for the eating thing?"

"He's not broken, Ty; he's strong, talented—"

"You're not listening to me," Tyler interrupted and handed me a card, which I took. "Call this guy, okay. He's a figure skater, you remember him?"

I turned the card in my hand, catching the rainbow face of it in the streetlamp's glow. *TRENT HANSON*. "I know who Trent Hanson is," I muttered. "Why do I need to call him?"

"To understand. *If* you really care about Kenji."

"I care. You know I do. He's…" What was he? An old friend? Someone I admired? Someone I was scared for? Fragile? Small in my arms. Soft, but tough.

Mine?

Tyler placed a hand on my arm, and this time, I didn't

shrug him off. "Promise me you'll call Trent, get some perspective; tell him how you feel about Kenji. That you want the best for him, and you're more than just friends."

I stiffened in shock. "I'm not into guys," I defended, and Tyler shrugged. Then, with no more words, he left to head back into the noodle place and Jonah.

And I turned the card over in my hands and felt so much weight on me I could have cried.

But I didn't.

Because I was a hockey player, who didn't show my emotions, wasn't at all gay, and wasn't wishing he could hold Kenji close and stop the world from hurting him.

Chapter Eight

Kenji

THE WEEK FOLLOWING THE NIGHT AT THE NOODLE shop was non-freaking-stop.

I had skate every morning, and Ilya was working us all incredibly hard. Anita left the ice in tears twice, and though she could be a witch at times, I felt sorry for her. We were all giving it as much as we had, and it was never quite enough. Sometimes, late at night when I was in bed, sore all over and half loopy from hunger, I wondered why I did it. Why was I skating? Why was I tormenting myself in a sport where only something like one out of fifty-thousand who tried made the Olympics. And that was the goal. Let's face it, if you didn't win gold at the Olympics in figure skating, no one knew who you were. I suspect most people—who weren't skating fanatics—could not name one figure skater who hadn't won a medal at the Olympics.

So yeah, those hard lonely nights made me doubt myself and my conviction to sports in general. Maybe Jun had the right idea. Be a nerd. No sprains, no bruises, no trainers yelling at you to be faster, tighter, thinner. Just books, books, and more books.

Yet, there were days when it all made some sort of mad, wonderful, agonizing sense. Those days were growing more and more distant. Today was one of those good days. Group had gone well. I weighed in at one-twenty on the nose. Ilya had nodded. Once. Then went off to gather the girls' weights from Anita who was in charge of jotting down the pounds lost or gained. I suspected the girls fudged things when needed. Lucky them. I wished I could do that, but I had Ilya hanging over my shoulder like a vulture.

Still, I had made goal weight. I felt good. Proud. The rest of the time went well. No one left the ice crying. There was a reason we have a space called kiss and cry, after all. Tears are a part of figure skating. I felt so good I approached Ilya after practice, my phone in my hand, my notes and music for a future routine to Dua Lipa's "One Kiss" all stored on the cell. Hell, I'd even sketched out a new outfit for the routine. All white and sparkly like the dress she wore in the song's video.

"Coach, can I have a minute?" I asked.

He glanced up from his notes, smoky eyes finding me over the top of his reading glasses. "Do you not have class?" he asked as he closed his tablet. The rink was empty now. The Coyotes would meet later today.

"I have some time." I sat beside him on the home team bench, my hands shaking as I gripped my phone. "So, the Snowflake Classic. I'd like to perform a routine that I choreographed for the exhibition program."

He studied me as if I were insane. "We have discussed this before, Kenji. Routines are prepared by me, for you. You are not a choreographer."

"I know, and I would never think to perform anything not cleared by you for the short or long programs. But this is just the exhibition after the competition. No points on the line. As you know." He continued to scrutinize me. "I know it's short notice," I hurried to say. "But my grandmother is already working on the outfit and—"

"That is presumptuous."

Shit. Shit. *Shit.* "Not at all." His stormy eyes narrowed. "If it was, I never meant it that way. I just wanted you to see that I am prepared. I've been working on this routine for months when I have free time. Can I just show it to you?"

"I will think on it. For now, you are to focus solely on the routines we have in place. Changing horses in the middle of the stream is poor practice and leads to confusion."

"No, no, I have no plans to change the routines. Never. We've worked too hard." He seemed to agree with that. "It's just some freestyle upbeat skating for the fans."

"Enough." I fell silent. "I will think on it. Is the music acceptable for juniors?"

"Totally. Can I send you a link to the song?"

"Yes, please. I will listen and judge if it is permissible. If it is, then perhaps we may add it to the exhibition routines, once we are sure the choreography is up to my standards."

I nearly flew to the ceiling like a balloon let off its string. "Thank you, Coach! Thank you."

With his gaze on my back, I floated to classes, then to lunch where I sat with the skater girls until I couldn't stand the snide shit and found a seat alone. I ate a few celery sticks, drank some skim milk, and trashed the rest of the food my mother had packed for me. I managed to avoid Shaun, or he was avoiding me, it was hard to say. I shouldn't have even cared, but my eyes betrayed me by searching for him in the halls between classes. No one filled out a frumpy school uniform finer than Shaun Stanton.

By the time I got home, I was struggling to make it through the door. My energy levels were low, and so was my sugar probably, so I needed to grab a nutrition shake from the fridge. When I shuffled through the front door, I was greeted by sheer chaos.

All of my mother's paintings—she created traditional Japanese watercolors that were so pretty sometimes my grandmother wept when she saw them—were now lined up in the living room. My dad had just rolled in from work, so he was still in uniform, and he and Sobo were standing in the middle of the paintings studying them.

"Uhm… what's going on?" I asked, dropping my book bag and skates to the floor. Mom gave me a look. I picked them up, then placed them on the sofa.

"Your mother has been chosen to show some of her art at the Susquehanna Art Museum as part of an Asian-American exhibition," Dad boasted.

Mom beamed. Sobo peeked up at me—which showed how tiny my grandmother was that she had to stare up at *me*—and reached out to pinch my cheek.

"Ow, Sobo, why?" I squealed.

"You look white," she said, pointed at a painting of a snowcapped mountain with a tiny pink pagoda sitting by a flamingo-colored lake, and told my mother to take that one. "You need something to eat."

"No, Sobo, I'm fine. Just going to grab a shake." I smiled at her, then fell into a long discussion with my mom and dad about what paintings to take. Everyone was flying high, the house so full of good vibes even Koro let me pet him. Once. Dinner was one of my favorites, my mother's beef stew, which I nibbled at, picking out the carrots and a few bits of beef.

"One of the other artists is a queer man, Mochi," Mom said as she passed me a bun, which I handed to my father. Dad ate like a horse. It was pretty obvious that I took after my mother. Petite, black hair, brown eyes. The only thing I got from my dad was my sense of humor, a love of history, and a freckle on my left earlobe.

"Oh cool!" I replied, warming inside at the family nickname for me. Mochi is a tiny frozen treat, a small ball of ice cream wrapped in dough. My dad started calling me that when I was born. Tiny, but sweet. And it just sort of stuck. I didn't mind. I'd heard much more embarrassing nicknames for other people. I could live with being a little-bitty tasty nugget of deliciousness. "So, I asked Coach if he would listen to my song for the exhibition skate that I came up with."

"And what did he say?" Mom asked, thumbing a strand of short ebony hair from her cheek. She wore it in a pixie cut that made her round face look amazing. She was so pretty. No wonder my dad had fallen for her when he saw her during his deployment in Japan. He said it was her artwork on the sidewalk that had captured him until he saw the artist, then he knew no mere paint on canvas could compare to the beauty that was Kiho Abiko. Old Kevin Kelly was a smooth one, that was for sure. A year later, Kiho Abiko became Kiho Kelly and shortly after that, they moved to the US, Dad retired from the Air Force, and they settled in Harrisburg to raise a family.

"He said he would think about it, which is beyond amazing with him," I stated as Sobo dunked her bun into her stew, then tried to make me take a bite. I waved it away, happy with the carrots, two bites of beef, and one chunk of potato I'd eaten. I probably should have skipped the spud, but I loved potatoes cooked with beef, so I indulged. I hoped that wouldn't bite me on the backside when we weighed in tomorrow morning. "So maybe he'll let me work it in. If not this year, then probs for sure next season."

"Way to go, son. It's good to see you being more

assertive with Ilya. I think he'll respect you for that," Dad, ever the macho flyboy pilot who had swept my mother off her tiny feet, replied as he helped himself to more stew. "So, this show is next weekend in Harrisburg. We're all going as a family to be with your mother. Jun is even pulling himself away from his studies for a few days. Rumor is, he may be bringing a friend."

"Don't make it sound as if the girl is anything other than a friend, Kevin. You know Jun isn't really into romancing people right now. He's putting all his energy into getting his masters."

Yeah, I strongly suspected my older brother was asexual, but kept that to myself. Sobo had enough trouble understanding bisexuality and pansexuality. I doubted she would be able to wrap her head around someone not having an interest in sex but longing for emotional intimacy. For most people, sex and love went hand in hand. I wasn't sure if my parents were feeling that Ace vibe from Jun or not. Mom might, but she was also keeping it to herself if she was.

"Right, yeah, but him bringing a girl home is something. He's always so wrapped up in his books. But, back on track. Would you like to bring a friend along to the showing as well? We have hotel rooms all lined up for the weekend, as well as an all-day pass to the civil war Civil War museum!"

"Oh cool!" I loved historical museums, no matter what the era. "Uhm…" I could only think of one other person who might enjoy a day spent among Civil War era exhibitions.

"They're even having a free Civil War dance class that weekend! I signed us up." Dad was about to bust his buttons.

"That is doubly cool!" I gushed.

"You two and your history," Mom giggled, then pointed her fork at me. "Why don't you invite Shaun? He loves history as much as you two do."

"That's a great idea, Kenji. We haven't seen Shaun much at all. I thought you two would rekindle your childhood friendship once we got you enrolled at Chesterford," Dad said as he speared a thick cube of tender beef.

"Well, we're both kind of busy, but… I don't know. I *guess* I could ask him." I shrugged and left that to dangle. Mom and Dad exchanged looks. Sobo slipped some meat to her cat who was under the table begging for scraps. No wonder he was such a porker.

I went to my room after dinner just to chill, study for a math test, and mull over the art show. Moving to my back as I lay on my bed, I stared at the ceiling as some new age meditation music flowed out of my phone. I let my eyes drift shut. My mind wandered down a few paths. All leading to Shaun Stanton. Was I still mad at him? I found that no, I wasn't, because Shaun was like everyone else who didn't quite get it. Sobo was always trying to stuff food at me or into me. I got it. Grandmothers always equated food with love. Maybe most people did, but food for me was a thing that needed to be kept under tight control.

Shaun should know that. Of all the people in the world, he should know. Yet, he kept trying to feed me. I didn't want his food—I wanted his friendship. Maybe even more than that, but he was straight, so that yearning was going to lead me nowhere. Still, we could be friends again. Maybe I was too sensitive. Ilya surely felt I was and did not hesitate to scold me about it, so perhaps the problem was me. More than likely so...

Sighing deeply, I rolled to my side, swiped the meditation app away and sent Shaun a text.

Kenji: *Hey, sorry about the noodle shop. I wasn't feeling well. ~K*

Kenji: *My folks wanted me to invite you to an art show/Civil War museum weekend if you're free next weekend? ~K*

Kenji: If not no biggie. Just figured you would be into it. ~K

Kenji: Civil War dancing bro. ~K

It took no time for me to see the dancing dots appear.

Shaun: Sorry about the noodle shop, too. I'm an asshole.

Shaun: Bro, you had me at Civil War dancing. ~S

———

PANTING AND LAUGHING, I FLOPPED DOWN BESIDE Shaun as my Mom and Dad began the Virginia Reel at the museum. We'd just done a hellacious couple of rounds of a quadrille.

"The folks back then were all kinds of scandalous," Shaun said with a nod to the period actors in flowing skirts and fancy vests who were showing the dance class participants the moves. "Look at all the hand-touching."

"Dude, they all have gloves on," I pointed out, then leaned back into the folding chair. The museum was open for us to investigate, and I was itching to check things out. "How scandalous can it be?" He chuckled. "Want to go check out the exhibits?"

"Yeah, I'd love that. You sure your folks won't

mind?" We both rose. Dad spied us, waved, and then, spun my mother around in a circle, which made her laugh.

"I think they're not seeing anything but each other," I said, then left the dancers to spin about in the bright March sun flowing through the windows of a large meeting room.

The lawn was soggy from melting snow., so the lessons took place inside. We'd already visited the cemetery where over a hundred and fifty Union and Confederate graves were located. That had been somber, and Shaun and I had been eager to leave the sadness behind.

The sound of fiddles, drums, and a fife followed us into the stately building. I could hear my mother's laughter for the longest time.

We meandered through the exhibits showcasing a range of Civil War era things like medical equipment, war memorabilia, and slavery that we both found upsetting and depressing.

Shaun made small talk as we made our way to the gift shop where we bought some replica Union caps to wear. Then, we made our way back into the museum to spend more time examining some of the artwork on the walls. One painting was of the war, cannons and bodies scattered about a bloody battlefield. Under the oil was a long gun, a musket, that seemed to be as long as I was tall.

"I wonder who the guy who lost this gun was," Shaun said as we stood side-by-side, our sight on the painting.

"I guess no one will ever know," I whispered, keeping my voice low out of respect for the artifacts and the guided tour taking place nearby.

He nodded, his gaze moving to grab mine. "I'm really sorry about the noodle shop, Kenji. I know food is a tricky subject for you." I tensed. "No, don't get mad. I just wanted to tell you that I realize that I tend to push too hard. I won't do that anymore. I swear."

"Okay, yeah..." I moved from the painting to sit on a bench. Shaun sat down beside me, his bulk filling the available space to my right. His thigh and mine were plastered together. The tour moved past. I stared down at my sneakers until they turned a corner. "I know you think I'm out of control like I was before, but I'm not."

"I never said you were out of control," he said softly, glancing my way from under the brim of his Union cap. "I never thought that at all. I just... what I saw that night..."

"I don't do that anymore." He nodded halfheartedly. "I don't. I only did that a few times. I saw a counselor. We got it under control. Everything is fine. I just have to stay lean for skating." He bit down on the inside of his cheek. "Seriously, I'm good. Strong. Healthy. You've seen me on the ice. Do I look out of control?"

"No, but you didn't look out of control when you were making yourself vomit."

I exhaled so hard it made my head feel funny. Guess I should have grabbed more breakfast at the hotel. My orange juice and cup of yogurt had been burned off by all the dancing.

"Look, I appreciate your concern, I do, but it's good. I talked to someone. I don't do that anymore. I promise."

"Okay, I believe you that you don't do that anymore, but you still—"

"No, please, don't start on me. You said you understood now."

"Sorry, yeah." He blew out a breath. "I won't preach. I just want to say that Ilya is using coaching methods from the freaking seventies or some other ancient era. He's fixating on weight, and that's not good, especially for kids our age, you know? You and the skater girls... I just..." He shrugged a thick shoulder. "I just worry. I care about you, Kenji. A lot."

He hooked his pinkie finger into mine. My heart did a triple lutz in my chest. I dared a peek and got lost in his bright blue eyes. He was looking at me in a way that was not that of a straight dude chatting with his bro. There was some real emotion in his gaze.

"I… care about you too," I whispered as we sat there across from some lost soldier's gun, pinkie fingers hooked, thighs tight to the other. It was the most romantic moment of my entire life. But was this really a romance thing? "Shaun, I mean…" I wiggled my pinkie finger. "Are you saying something to me here, with this?" I lifted our joined fingers into the air.

He stared at our hands for the longest minute ever recorded.

"I think I might be…"

"It's cool. You don't have to say another thing. I'll totally keep your secret if what this means is what I think it might mean."

He cleared his throat, bobbed his head, and we said nothing more about the pinkie hold that went on for about forty minutes.

Guess there were times when words just got in the way.

Chapter Nine

Shaun

I ENDED THE CALL AND SAT THERE, THE WEIGHT OF Trent's words lingering heavily on my mind. His words about the pressures of being a figure skater from a young age, and how it can lead to eating disorders, hit close to home. I had messaged him the day after the noodle shop disaster, and he'd messaged me back right away, saying he'd call me next weekend. I'd never expected him to call, but I'd dropped Soren's name, and given Soren was Ten's son, and Ten played hockey with Dieter, who was married to Trent, well... I let out a sigh... yeah, he called back, and now I didn't know what to do with myself.

I held hands with Kenji.

I held his hand.

I looked out the window, my thoughts wandering to Kenji, especially since Trent had mentioned what he thought Kenji might be going through. An eating disorder, a mental block to eating at all, anorexia nervosa. It was the last thing that scared me the most because that was a word I knew. Trent said he'd seen this before in figure skating, the fear of gaining weight and a distorted body image leading to a significant restriction of food intake. Everything fit, and I couldn't shake the image of Kenji, his discomfort obvious as he'd taken nothing more than a few sips of soup. I hadn't realized that he was fighting some unseen battle, one I couldn't fully understand, but Trent made it obvious.

He said it could be other things, that he wasn't a specialist, but he spoke about image, and strength, and a whole ton of things I couldn't get my head around. The tension in Kenji's shoulders when I'd made him eat at the noodle shop, the haunted expression—it was all too real, too raw. And as much as I wanted to help him, to be his ally in this fight, I realized the last thing he needed was for me to add to that battlefield.

No more forcing him to eat. No more mentioning

the time way back that I'd caught him making himself sick. No more anger at him putting figure skating before himself.

So, what did I do now?

My phone vibrated with a message, one that Trent had promised me, a link to resources and to a couple of therapists he recommended.

Then, another message, summarizing everything Trent had said about what I could do. *Just be his friend. I'll talk to Ilya.* My heart hitched. Even though Trent promised he wouldn't mention Kenji, that it would just be a general chat about up-and-coming figure skaters and the pressure to be perfect, I was still worried. What if Ilya worked it out and said something to Kenji, and then Kenji knew what I'd done and…

Shit, I'm hyperventilating. This is too much.

I could be his friend. That is what he needs now.

I didn't have to think about the warmth in me whenever I looked at him, or thought about him, or worried about him.

Or held his hand.

We'd been friends before he'd chosen figure skating and I stayed in hockey, before we'd drifted away from each other. Was I being stupid? I mean, we'd been kids when we'd bonded over being out on the ice, and what if Kenji didn't need a friend like me right now?

He'd invited me to the history and art thing, that was kind, that was us being friends, and I'd been honest with him that there was something inside me that I wanted to share with him. I could be a friend who supported him with the eating disorder and the stress I saw in his face, and he could hold my hand if I came out of the closet. The thought of having someone in my corner who knew me was enough for me to smile.

I headed into Mom's room, pulled down the scrapbook she kept on the top shelf, my mum's way of collecting all kinds of hockey-related things on my way to the NHL—Dad's wording, not mine or my mom's. Then I returned to my room before anyone could catch me not doing the homework I'd said I had to do. The glitter on its cover caught the light as I opened to the first page, me being held by my dad in the hospital, in my Toronto jersey, him beaming proudly. He seemed softer in these photos, not so determined to live vicariously through me, still working hard at the AHL level and hoping to get seen.

He never got seen.

And now, he didn't seem to smile much at all.

I flipped the pages and memories flooded back as I scanned through the photos, images frozen in time from my days on the ice, and there it was, aged five, Kenji and me, full-caged face masks off, in the teeniest tiniest hockey gear ever.

I photographed every image or Kenji, his familiar grin and determined gaze staring back at me from the glossy paper. With each photo I took, I smiled harder.

Then, grabbing my keys, I tried to head out without getting caught, which didn't happen like that at all. As I passed through the living room, Mom caught me.

"Heading out, sweetheart?"

"Library," I lied and pressed a quick kiss to her cheek. I almost made it outside, but Dad was out of his study in an instant and blocking my way.

"Where are you off to?"

"Library," I replied, trying to keep my tone casual. "Need some resources for homework."

"Why don't you use Google like normal kids do?" he grouched, eyeing my backpack.

Since when was I normal? He'd made sure I would never be *completely* normal. "I need access to archives."

He had nothing to say about my education, aside from knowing how low my grades could go before I lost my place on the team. Luckily for me and him, I was a straight-A student—well, A and a few B-pluses —and for the most part, it was easy enough to stay in everyone's good books, school, and home both. Head down, work hard.

He frowned. "We still have that Arizona-LA game tape to watch," he insisted, a hint of frustration creeping into his voice. He insisted on us watching tapes of old games, acting as if this was some normal father/son thing, when actually, all he did was shout at the games and disparage them, as well as criticize me.

"I'll catch up on it later," I promised, already halfway out of the door. "I need to get this done."

With that, I escaped, stepping out into the crisp morning air, a sense of determination pushing me forward. There was something more important than game tape waiting for me. There was step one in the Kenji-is-my-best-friend-again-and-I-will-help-him plan.

I needed to come up with a catchier title. Oh, and ignore hand-holding, or the urge to cradle him close and kiss him. Nope, that would be bad. I was in the closet—he was a bright shining star—we didn't fit in that way.

The bell above the door of the photography store chimed, announcing my arrival to the clerk, who looked up from behind the counter with a friendly smile. I went over to the print machine, but there was a big *Out-of-Order* notice, and some of my happy bubbles popped.

"I need to print out some photos," I replied, reaching into my pocket to pull out my phone. "Just a few from my gallery."

He brightened. "No worries. If you can upload them to the store account, we can bypass the machine, and I can do that for you directly." He slid a card over the counter with an email address and code. I selected the images I needed and sent them.

"Got it," he said, flashing me a quick grin before disappearing into the back room. I shifted on my feet, my stomach twisting with nerves and anticipation—was this going to work? They were probably shitty quality. A few minutes later, he returned with a stack of glossy prints in hand, each one a snapshot of memories, and I thanked him, my voice catching in my throat as I took the photos from him.

Only one of them was blurred, but I could handle that another day.

This might be stupid anyway—I mean, who even printed out photos these days? I headed to the stationery place, picked up a scrapbook, all the while considering whether I should send them to him on his socials.

Clutching the photos, scrapbook, and glue, I headed to the library and found a table at the back behind the romance section. Then, I made a scrapbook for him, all about us, of the times we'd been friends, the games, the Peewee stuff, the frozen pond at the house down the road, the first sparkly leotard he'd worn, the sad face I pulled next to his grinning one, me with a stick, him with his arms stretched up like a ballerina.

Back then, I knew he wouldn't be playing hockey, and that, maybe, we wouldn't see each other all the time. I never imagined we would drift apart or end up fighting.

I'm going to fix that.

As soon as the scrapbook was done, I doodled our names on the cover—not quite as sparkly as my mom's one—and debated adding some hearts because he was my friend and I loved him.

That was all. Right? The weird fluttering in my chest whenever I saw him, the desperate pull to touch him, was nothing but friendship because I couldn't let it be anything else.

Anyway, hearts were probably overkill, right?

Then, I logged in to the library's internet and

started my research from the links Trent had sent me. I wasn't going home yet—knowing how I could help Kenji was more important than watching game films.

Kenji was more important than hockey.

MONDAY ARRIVED ALL TOO SOON, THE SHRILL SOUND of my alarm jolting me awake, but I rolled out of bed, my heart already pounding with anticipation and nerves. Today was important. I was going to be the best friend in the entire world, so Kenji could trust me, and then, I'd fix things.

Grabbing a bagel from the kitchen, I barely paused to chew as I hurried out the door, and was at the rink by 5:30, hurrying to the changing rooms. I shed my street clothes and pulled on my practice gear, but as I laced up my skates, my hands were unsteady with nerves, the weight of all my plans making my head hurt. By 5:40, I was out on the ice, my skates gliding over the smooth surface. Kenji was already there, stretching at his end of the rink, his movements fluid and precise. His choice of attire—pink leggings and a purple shirt—was just Kenji. I wanted to go back to the locker room, grab the scrapbook, and shove it at him, showing him the first time that he'd dressed up to dance on the ice.

He glanced over at me, a smile lighting his face. A surge of warmth spread through my chest. Despite the early hour and the chill in the air, there was nowhere else I'd rather be than here on the ice, with Kenji down at his end, as we worked on our skills, no one else there.

Of course, that changed as soon as Ilya arrived, angry and loud, and snapping out something about Kenji's lines being wrong. Fuck him—Kenji was good out there. Still, Kenji didn't argue, nodded, changed whatever he was doing, and I pretended not to be watching. Which was a good thing because then, my dad arrived, grumpy and snapping that I hadn't set out the cones right.

I was done with both of them.

By the time I made it to the locker room, Kenji was out of the shower and knotting his tie ready for the school day, and he sketched a wave as he left. I couldn't go over to him smelling as bad as I did, so I showered, headed to school, sat through Geography, and a boring and frustrating Math class, and it was lunchtime before I tracked Kenji down, finding him at his usual table on the opposite side of the room to the hockey guys. When I caught him glancing up at me, I pretended not to have noticed the lonely apple on his tray.

"Can we talk?" I asked, and the buzz of chat at his table died. "I have something to show you."

Someone snickered about jocks, but Kenji shot them a glare, and they subsided. He picked up his apple to follow me, and we headed outside, finding a table behind the drama block, and then, I put my best-friends-again-so-I-can-help plan into action.

And yep, I *really* needed to think of a cooler name.

Chapter Ten

Kenji

Seeing Shaun being so secretive made me feel a little wary.

What could he possibly want to show me? If it was something about teenagers and food, I was going to—

"So, I know this isn't as fancy as the ones that all the moms all over the world make, but I thought it might be... I don't know... nice?" He pulled something out of his backpack, something big. "I know there's supposed to be lace and shit around the edges, and the front and back are supposed to be fabric-covered, but I didn't have any lace or fabric, so

I left it as it was." He passed over a scrapbook. One that he must have gotten from a dollar store kids' aisle because it was the most glittery, unicorn-laden thing I had ever seen.

I took the offering, letting it rest on my open palms. The March wind was cold, a sign that winter was not quite ready to let go of Pennsylvania just yet. I shivered but wasn't sure if it was from the brisk winds rolling through the quad or the fact that Shaun had made me this amazing gift. With his own big hands. Didn't matter what was inside it. The fact that he'd sat down and done this, for me, was… well, it made me teary.

"No, oh shit, did I do something wrong?" He was at my side in an instant, standing over me as if he could protect me from all the wrongs in the world.

I shook my head, sniffled, then turned my face into his chest, the scrapbook now pressed between us. His arm came around me, stiffly at first, his palm landing on my back with a thud. I snorted at his fumbling attempt to console me.

"You did so good," I coughed out, my nose buried in his Chesterford jacket. He smelled of fabric softener and some sort of dark woodsy cologne. "I'm not sure why I'm being such a tool," I said into the soft material covering his wide chest.

His pats began to soften as I sniveled. Softer, less a whack and more a caress. I melted into him as much as I dared in front of the braver students.

"Maybe we should go inside?" he asked as my sniffles quieted.

I nodded, stepping away from his warmth. He studied my face, sapphire eyes filled with concern. Always such a worrier. Even when we were kids Shaun was the one who would fret over everything and everyone. Which made him an excellent captain and friend.

"Your cheeks will get chapped being all wet." He used his thumbs to dry the dampness from my cheeks. I yearned to rise to my toes to kiss his soft lips. I nearly did when someone dashed past, shouting about the wind coming off a glacier. Some random dude, no idea who, but it was enough to snap the mood in two like a wishbone. Oh man, did I have a few wishes swirling around inside my head. "Come on," Shaun said, plucking my apple from the table, then steering me into the drama building.

Which seemed kind of fitting to me. Shaun and I were the epitome of teen drama. For real, we could be leads in one of those John Hughes movies my parents were so fond of. We slipped into the wardrobe room; the heat felt good as we settled on an old steamer trunk amid racks of costumes from past performances.

"Sorry for that outburst," I whispered, peering down at the scrapbook now resting on my thighs. "I've been kind of whirly ever since we had our pinkie moment."

He made a sound that reminded me of a sad puppy. Not exactly a whine, but something soft and plaintive. I let my head rest on his shoulder.

"I'm really confused right now, Kenji," he confessed, his words mere puffs of a whisper.

"I know," I replied as we sat there side by side, the smell of mothballs thick on the air. "You can talk to me anytime. Discovering things about yourself that you didn't know before is really hard."

"I think I knew it," he said, his thigh solid and strong beside mine. "Like, I knew I had feelings for you that were more than just friendship. I don't think I feel this way about anyone else."

My heart soared. "That's… you're so sweet. I feel the same."

And I let it drop. I didn't want to push him. This was big for him. Huge. He had to do this at his own pace. "So, let's travel back in time?" I patted the rainbow-bright cover and chanced a peek to the left.

He was watching me, his lips flat until our eyes met. Then, he smiled. It was wobbly, but still breathtaking. I opened the book. Glued to the page was a picture of us when we were little guys. We looked lost inside our hockey gear. I chuckled. "Oh man, I was so tiny."

"You're still tiny," he remarked.

Yeah, that was true. Compared to him, I was a sprite.

"Hulking guys on skates play hockey, and tiny guys on skates dance on ice," I threw out as I flipped the page to another old snapshot of us, maybe a year past the first, Shaun already six inches taller than me at the age of ten or so. I was in a skating costume in this one. I remembered it well. A bright yellow top with slim black slacks. I'd won a medal at my first competition, third place, just a bronze, but that win had been the thing that had led me from hockey to figure skating. It had lit a fire in me to combine the ice with fluidity and music. A fire I had been sure would never burn out. Now though…

"That's not always true. There are some small guys who play hockey. Lots of pros are under six-foot-tall. Size means nothing," he quickly countered.

"That's what all the giants say," I teased.

He saw me smirking and chuffed in amusement.

"Do you remember what I said to you when you told me you were done with hockey?"

"Sure. You said that the ice would always be a part of me, no matter if I were chasing pucks or spinning around like a top. That once you put skate blade to frozen water you were never the same. It was pretty profound for a kid of ten."

He blushed. "I wish I could say it was my words, but I kind of skimmed them from Tennant Rowe. I'd seen an interview with him when he first joined the Railers, way before he got married and became a dad. He was talking about how the ice was a magical thing, that when your blade met it for the first time it captured your heart. I wanted you to know that even though I was going to miss you on the hockey team that... well, that I wanted you to be happy."

He glanced away from me, his gaze going to a rack of medieval outfits. Feeling my emotions rising again, I grew bold. I chanced leaning up to place my lips to his cheek. His cheek was soft, the blond whiskers freshly shaved. His breath skipped as he inhaled.

"You are the kindest soul that I have ever known," I told him before returning to the scrapbook.

Another page turned. Shaun sat beside me, silent, his cheeks pink, his gaze darting from the pages with the old images, some plastered in sideways, some with tacky fingerprints where the glue had coated his fingers. Time felt as if it had stopped for us, but time runs on no matter how much we wish we could sit in a costume closet forever. The first bell rang.

"Shit, I have to get across campus to the Science building for Biology. Mr. Harrison loves handing out detention for being late."

"He's a dick. He got me twice already this semester. I have him first, and he has no interest in hearing about hockey as an excuse for being tardy. Tardy. Who even uses that word anymore?"

"Mr. Harrison because he's ten thousand years old and eats garlic on his Wheaties," I tossed out as we got to our feet. "Thanks for showing this to me."

I held out the scrapbook. "No, that's for you. I made it for you because…" He stared down at me as a hundred feelings cavorted behind his eyes. "Because I want to be your friend again."

"Only friends?" I asked, knowing I shouldn't have. I just wanted to be more than that to him.

"No." The word left him on an exhalation. He bent down to kiss me on the forehead. A fast peck that made my empty stomach swoop as if I were on a roller coaster. I blinked in shock. He smiled, then pressed the apple into my chest. "Eat that."

Before I could reply, he threw open the door. Students were passing by, voices loud, laughter filling the room. A few curious eyes found us before moving past.

"Thank you for the memories," I said while stepping out into the flow of teenagers hustling from lunch or other classes to where they needed to be next.

"You're welcome. We'll make lots of new ones for all the empty pages at the back, yeah?"

Second bell rang. The kids around me started hustling. "Yeah, lots of new ones."

We both took off in different directions. Me to try to beat the closing door of Mr. Harrison's science lab, and Shaun to whatever the rest of the day held for him.

I hoped he got to his class on time. I didn't. Dick Bag Harrison nailed me with a detention, which was going to piss Ilya off to no end. Still, it would let me spend an hour after school thumbing through the scrapbook in my backpack. Felt like a fair trade to me.

SHAME MY COACH DID NOT SHARE MY THOUGHTS about detention and old pictures of best buddies.

Ilya was livid when I texted him to let him know that I was in detention and would miss group skate. I was told to report to the rink after detention, and we would work privately. The mere thought of seeing him when he was in a temper made me sick to my stomach.

The apple I'd tossed into the trash on my way to science probably would have come back up if I'd eaten it. So, good thing I hadn't.

Ilya was at the rink waiting when I showed up, slinking in like a beaten-up tom cat who'd been out carousing for a week. I began to apologize but was shut down.

"I do not need excuses. If you had stayed home schooling, as I recommended, this delay would not have happened."

"I'm sorry," I whimpered as I rushed to lace up my skates. "I'll do better."

"Sorry does not win medals. Work wins medals. Dedication to your sport wins medals. Now, get on the ice before I remove your name from my list of students. Perhaps, that is what you are wishing for?"

I paused in tying my skate to stare at him in confusion. "No, Coach. I know you are the best trainer and choreographer that I could have."

His gray eyes burned into me as he stood on the

ice, arms folded over his thick sweater. "Are you sure? Perhaps you should reconsider discussing my methods with your silly friends, who then tell other people of how we train. Then, those people call me up with idiotic American ideals on how to teach belligerent, ungrateful children who show up late to practice ten days before a competition!"

"I'm sorry," I repeated, not a clue as to what had him so pissed off. "I have no idea what you mean, Coach. I never talk about your methods."

"You are also a liar." He bent down to place his hands on my shoulders, his gaze hot with indignation. It was more than a little scary. "The next time you go whining to another coach about how you are treated by me, you can become their student. Then, you can languish away in some miserable rink with the rest of the boys who do not know how good they have got it. Do we understand each other, Kenji Kelly?"

"Sir, yes, I won't... I didn't say anything to any other coach. I swear."

He released me then, turning his back to me. "You will perform the long, short, and exhibition programs that I have designed for you at the Snowflake Classic. There will be no deviations."

"Yes, Coach," I mumbled under my breath while he skated to the sound system to cue up my music. No deviations. That meant I was not allowed to perform the routine I'd choreographed. Shaking with fear and anger, I hit the ice for what I knew would be a grueling hour of jumps repeated so many times my muscles would let me down.

And they did. Over and over. As I sat on the ice, sore and wobbly with Ilya shouting at me to get to my skates, I felt out of control. The tears began to flow. Ilya called me a soft mewling baby, then told me to go home to my mommy, his ire still bubbling like a caldera.

He left then. Just stormed out of the rink, my music still playing, me still seated mid-ice with wet cheeks and trembling hands. Home seemed a million miles away. Everything good and kind, like Shaun and my family and my ability to perform a simple routine I had done a dozen times already, so far out of my grasp that they all might as well be on Mars.

Mars…

I swiped at my face as a memory popped into my head. It was bold and bright, unlike the other thoughts swirling around my skull. Shaun and me when we were perhaps eight, sitting on the bench during a morning practice, the seats behind us filled with groggy parents. Our coach had handed out fun-size candy bars as he always did as a treat for a good practice.

Shaun and I both had Mounds bars. If I closed my eyes, I could taste the sweet coconut covered with chocolate. Mm, it had been forever since I'd had a candy bar. Candy was off-limits.

Shaking, I got to my skates and made my way to the Coyotes bench, my mind set on finding a fucking Mounds bar. I had none in my bag, I knew that, but my sloppy brain made me search. Once that proved futile, I took off my skates, tied up my sneakers, and left the rink with my skates over one shoulder and my overstuffed backpack on the other.

The air was cold, the sky now ominous as I pushed myself into a jog. The campus fell behind me. I felt the bite of sleet on my cheeks as I made my way past the Noodle Shop to a small convenience store/gas station. Winter was not giving up meekly. I hurried into the store, my stomach growling as the smell of the hot dogs on the roller-thingy in the corner reached my nose. I didn't want hot dogs. I wanted a Mounds bar.

I found the candy aisle, grabbed a dozen candy bars, and then, a soda, too. A big one. Huge. Something else that Ilya forbade his skaters to drink. Water. Water was all a body needed. Americans and their fixation on junk food showed weak moral constitution.

"Fuck you, Ilya," I grumbled as I made my way to the register. Once the goodies were mine, I stepped outside, sat on the windowsill with a flashing green lotto light illuminating me in the sleety gray evening, and ingested every single candy bar I had purchased. They were delicious. *So, fucking delicious*. And the soda that followed to wash them down? Fucking incredible. Sweet, filled with fizz and sugar. I belched a few times, loud, and then giggled at the sound.

I walked back to my car, coat pockets filled with wrappers I would have to get rid of somewhere secret. A dumpster maybe? I was soaked, chilled to the bone, and feeling terrible about the amount of food I had just eaten.

My car was locked, and so, I shrugged my backpack off my shoulder to dig my keys out. Remembering the junk in my pockets, I tossed the garbage into the car to take care of later. Where was a dumpster I could sneak this into? My reflexes were dulled, and the bag hit the wet blacktop of the student parking lot. Everything inside tumbled out. My books, my phone, and the scrapbook.

"No, fucking goddamn it!" I railed at the wintry sky, falling to my knees to gather the scrapbook up before it was ruined. I couldn't handle that. I cradled it to my chest, the sleet pelting down on my head, tiny pebbles of ice melting under my knees and soaking my skate pants through in no time. My phone buzzed. I looked down at it lying beside my front tire. Everything was spiraling around and around like a drain. I'd eaten so much bad food. Thousands of calories. Weigh-in tomorrow would be horrific. My phone continued to vibrate.

I glanced at the incoming call. Shaun. What... why? I sat in the parking lot, scrapbook tight to my chest, the urge to purge so strong I was shivering violently. My fingers were cold, shaking, and wet. I picked up my cell, held it to my ear, and said hello.

"Hey, we're at the noodle shop and everyone on the team is asking where you are. You want to come have some broth with us?"

I was in no place to sit and be stared at by our friends. I just wanted to see Shaun.

"Shaun..." I pushed out, unable to form the denial to his request for some reason. "Can you... I think... will you come to student parking, please? I don't feel... I need you."

"I'll be there in five," he replied, and I could hear a chair scraping across a tile floor as he rushed to stand. Voices asking him if he was okay. Him saying he had to go. The ring of the bells over the Hot Pot Noodle Shop door as he bolted out into the rotten weather. He was coming. I could hold on until he got here. Shaun was coming. The book was safe. It would be okay. I could do this. I could hold on for Shaun.

Chapter Eleven

Shaun

My heart skipped a beat when Kenji answered my call. Anticipation bubbled within me, and I grinned. Only, as soon as I answered and heard Kenji's voice, the warmth drained from my veins, replaced by a cold, gnawing fear.

"Shaun... Can you... I think... Will you come to student parking, please? I don't feel right... I need you."

Without a second thought, I rushed out of the door into the cold, my mind spinning with worry and uncertainty. I hadn't stopped to explain why I was leaving, a knot forming in the pit of my stomach, twisting, and tightening with each syllable he'd managed to force out. I knew something was wrong, terribly wrong. When I reached the parking lot, I scanned the rows of cars frantically, searching for any sign of Kenji. And then, there he was, a solitary figure huddled on the ground, leaning against the tire of his Jetta, slumped with his head bowed, his bag clutched to his chest. I sprinted the short distance, a surge of relief washing over me at the sight of him. But when I drew closer, my steps thundering on the sidewalk, he lifted his head, and when I skidded to a stop, his eyes were clouded with pain, and his usual vibrant energy was dimmed.

"Kenji?" I gasped, dropping to my knees beside him. "What's wrong? What happened? Did someone hurt you?"

I would kill them, or at least knock anyone out who hurt him, and I even scanned the local area for assailants, but there was no one, just Kenji curled in on himself. I couldn't look away as he struggled to catch his breath, trembling with a panic attack.

"Shaun…" he managed, then hid his face in his hands.

"What happened?" I asked, my voice tinged with worry as I reached out to brush the hair from his forehead, feeling him shaking.

Was he cold? I slipped off my coat, attempted to

tuck it around him, ignoring the icy pellets of rain bouncing off my back. Before I could utter another word, he stared up at me, his eyes red, his face blotchy, reaching blindly for my hand, and gripping it tight.

"I can't control it, Shaun," he gasped, his words rushed and frantic. "It's like... something else takes over, and I can't stop myself." His words sent a shiver down my spine, a cold dread settling in the pit of my stomach. What had he done? Was it pills? Drugs? What was he doing? My mind raced with a whirlwind of questions and uncertainties, each one more terrifying than the last. The sight of Kenji huddled and trembling, his face pale and drawn with anguish, filled me with a sense of urgency unlike anything I had ever felt before. Was I overreacting?

"We need to get you out of the rain," I managed, attempting to keep my voice low. Did I need to call 911? Did he need medical help?

"I'm so sorry," he cried and scrubbed at his face so hard I thought he might hurt himself. I caught his hands to stop him. "I'm so ugly; I can't jump... I..." He stopped, and a fresh bout of sobs caught me unawares.

"Kenji? Did you take pills? Do I need to get paramedics?"

"No!" He yelled at me, then shoved at me. "No!" I tumbled back from my crouch down on my ass, and then, he launched himself at me. "I'm sorry! I'm sorry!" I caught him, and pulled him onto my lap, so small in my arms, burying his face in my shirt, which was wet from the melting sleet.

"Shaun?" Tyler asked from behind me, and I glanced up to see him and a couple of the other guys staring down. "What can we do?"

I shook my head. I didn't know.

"I'm going to get him home." I said, and Tyler nodded. I unpeeled the keys from Kenji's icy fingers. "He'll be okay. He has the flu," I lied.

Tyler nodded, although I knew he didn't believe me. "The flu, yeah. Do you want me to take him home?"

I scrambled to stand, thanking anyone who listened that I had good lower body strength as I carried Kenji up with me, Tyler holding my hand to steady me. Did I want to hand Kenji to Tyler, or Soren, or Felix, or any one of the team hanging around me?

"I've got this. I'll look after him."

Tyler made a motion for everyone else to leave, then leaned into me. "Has he eaten anything?" I pointed down at the wrappers on the ground, candy, and the ginormous bottle of soda.

Tyler paled. "He binged all that?" he murmured for me to hear. I shrugged. It could be anyone's trash, but when Tyler picked it all up, I knew it was Kenji's.

Tyler took the keys and unlocked the car. I managed to separate Kenji from his bag after a short tussle, then I helped Kenji into the passenger seat, and he didn't protest once, or say a word, he cried and gripped me and wouldn't let go.

"I need to drive you back home," I whispered, close to Kenji's ear.

He raised dark eyes swimming with tears. "Don't tell anyone. Please, don't tell them."

I pressed a kiss to the top of his head and squeezed his hand. "I won't say a thing."

He closed his eyes, sinking in his seat, and I hurried to the driver's side, taking back the keys, and bumping Tyler's fist.

"I've got this," I said to him.

Tyler glanced inside at Kenji. "I know. I can help if you need me. Call me, okay?"

I said I would, and when I was inside with the door shut, I turned on the engine and waited for it to warm. Kenji's place was about fifteen minutes from here, and I hoped it was enough time so I could get some heating inside the car to counteract the chill. I turned to check on him one last time, but as I reached out to touch his shoulder, he flinched, his gaze distant and troubled.

By the time we reached his place, a modest middle-class home, he was calmer, lucid, and as soon as the car stopped, he fumbled with the door to let himself out.

"Thank you," he said, shaking the handle, frustration seeping into his movements when he couldn't open the door, and I was around there in an instant, helping him out, grabbing his bag. "Thank you," he repeated. "I'm okay now." It didn't sound like Kenji. It sounded like a stranger giving me a polite brush-off, and if he thought for one minute I was leaving, he was wrong.

Kenji's mom opened the door, her smile of welcome dropping when she saw me propping up Kenji.

"Kenji!" she exclaimed and reached for him, but he evaded her touch by burying himself in my hold.

"It's just food poisoning," he murmured.

"What did you eat? Was it that noodle place again?" Her voice was filled with fear and anger at whoever might have hurt Kenji, and she was talking and worrying like moms do as I helped Kenji inside.

His weak explanation of food poisoning had pushed his mom into mama-bear mode, but she wasn't any bigger than him, and there was no way she'd get him upstairs to the room I recalled from when I used to visit.

"I'll get him upstairs, stay with him for a while," I said, and his mom shot me a glance.

"The kind of thing a boyfriend might do," Kenji's grandmother—his sobo—announced from the kitchen doorway. "Are you his boyfriend, little Shaun?"

Coming out and declaring a romantic relationship with Kenji without his consent was disrespectful, right? It wasn't fair to lump myself on him, and anyway, no one needed to know I was gay in a situation like this. Why add complications to an already stressful moment. I met his sobo's shrewd gaze.

"I'm his friend. A close friend. His best friend."

"You haven't been around much," Kenji's mom added, nearly tripping over Koro as the cat wound through her legs. She shut the front door behind us, when Kenji, me, and Kenji's grandmother were locked in this weird closeted gay standoff.

Sobo sniffed, muttered something under her breath. "Either way, you go up, his door stays open."

His mom bustled around, aiding us in removing

our shoes with flustered movements, breaking the calm atmosphere I was trying to maintain. Kenji thanked me once more when we reached his room, again he was expecting me to leave, but I couldn't bring myself to walk away, not when he needed someone by his side.

Not when I needed to hear the whole story.

"The worst of the sickness is over," I assured his mom, my voice steady. "I'll stay with him for a while; maybe we can watch a movie or something."

I waited for Kenji to answer, but instead, he moved the short distance between me and his bed and sat on the side. I pulled up a chair beside him, determined to stay there until he was feeling better. Whatever had caused this despair—why he'd maybe eaten all that junk food and the soda—I was going to be there for him. I wouldn't even ask questions, but maybe, he'd trust me enough to tell me everything. His mom vanished, then came back with water and snacks.

"For you," she said as she placed a plate of crackers on the bedside cabinet. Then, she pressed the back of her hand to Kenji's forehead, tutted, fussed around him, and pressed a kiss to his hair, the same as I'd done in the car.

We both cared for him.

She loved him.

And I…

Well, I loved him, too. In my own way. As his friend. As someone who'd grown up knowing him, and seeing him, and sharing all kinds of secrets, caring, and worrying, and watching out for him as he watched out for me. He was the person who understood how I felt about the pressure my dad heaped on me, about how hard I worked to be good. I understood his drive to be the best.

And after all of our shared moments, we'd come back together as friends, and he'd answered the phone when I called. He was having a panic attack, but he'd wanted me to help.

"Is she gone?" he asked, his voice muffled because he'd buried his face in a pillow.

"Yeah."

He turned, groaning as he moved, small and unhappy, tears still collecting in his eyes. "I need my bag," he said, and I passed it to him, wiping at the damp parts. He took it from me, clumsy as he attempted to open it at speed, then yanking out the contents, picking up the scrapbook I'd made and opening each page in silence. The cover was wet, but the photos were okay inside, and he traced each one, using his quilt cover to dab at the damp parts.

"I could have… I didn't…" he tried to talk, but then, he stopped when none of the words were stringing together to make any sense.

"What happened?" I asked, and his eyes widened as he clutched the scrapbook to his chest. Tears spilled down his face, and I moved from the chair to sit on the side of his bed, touching his hand. "Kenji?"

"I can't," he whispered brokenly. "Don't make me say anything about it to you."

I got the sense that he didn't want to talk to me, but maybe someone else? "Would you like to talk to Tyler? Or—"

"No!"

We sat in silence for a while, and I hadn't moved my hand from his arm. He was exhausted, his eyelids dipping every so often, and he leaned toward me. For a while, we sat like that, until I eased him away, swung my legs up onto the bed and settled back on the pillows, pulling him to me, unpeeling his fingers from the scrapbook, then reaching for the control and flicking on Netflix. I found an old anime we used to love and set it going. He didn't move from my hold, and all too soon, his breathing evened out, and he fell asleep in my arms.

I sent a message to Mom to tell her I'd be late home, another message to Tyler explaining that Kenji was okay, and it didn't surprise me when Kenji's sobo appeared at the open door. She considered me in her great and wise way, then smiled.

"Are you his boyfriend?" she repeated her earlier question.

I wished I had an answer. "I don't know if I can be," I whispered, as Kenji shifted in my arms and sighed in his sleep. I glanced down at him, hugged him closer, then eased away, tucking him into his quilt, aware she was watching me. I stopped next to her, and she reached up and patted my face.

"Are you his boyfriend?" she whispered.

I glanced at a sleeping Kenji, then took the seat next to the bed. The answer was important to her, and just as important to me. Then, I slumped a little as she smiled up at me. I really had only one answer.

I want to be.

Chapter Twelve

Kenji

Sleep was like a dark cloud of nothingness.

No dreams, no sounds, no images lurking in the shadows. It was as if my brain had closed up shop for the duration. What woke me up was a strong shudder racking my body. It felt like one of those all-body quakes that hit right before you fall ill. Like the first tremors that strike telling you, yep, I think I'm coming down with something. I blinked awake. My damp clothes clung to me, warm, but still wet. A strong pair of arms held me. I knew without tipping my head back that it was Shaun clasping me to him. His scent enveloped me at the same time as his arms did, and I loved it. It made things right in a world that was becoming horribly wrong.

"Hey," he whispered. That one word vibrating through his chest. "Are you awake?"

"Mm," I moaned, unwilling to speak or move.

"You're shivering," he said, his hold on me remaining steadfast, yet I knew if I asked him to let go, he would. But I didn't want him to let go. Not ever.

"Wet clothes," I mumbled into his hoodie, the soft cotton well-worn.

It was a plush, comforting cloth, like a favored blankie from childhood. I'd had one once, flannel, and I'd carried it everywhere until it started to fray. Sobo had taken the blanket one day as I wailed and turned it into a teddy bear. The tears had stopped as I watched the yellow-and-blue checkered toy come to life. Sobo was one hell of a seamstress. I still had Teddy. He sat on my dresser, ragged, and stained, watching over me as a good friend would. Just like Shaun.

"Oh shit, okay, yeah, you need to get out of those and shower."

"Are you trying to see me naked?" I teased, the humor falling flat as I felt as though I'd been tied to a caboose, then dragged all the way to Canada.

"Kenji, no, I would never," Shaun gasped. I lifted my head to find his gaze on me. "Never while you were sick," he corrected softly.

"Someday, I want to see you naked," I whispered.

"The door is open," he pointed out. "And your grandmother keeps passing by like a sentry guard every ten minutes."

"Ugh," I groaned, pushing to one arm to rest on my elbow. He looked so good lying on my bed, his hair sticking up after drying from the wintry mess we'd been in. The cold, biting memory of my weakness poked at me, the guilt and shame like a knife between the ribs. Ilya was right. I was a weakling.

"Hey, are you okay? You suddenly went all kinds of pale," he asked, concern darkening his blue gaze.

"I'm fine." I lied right to his face. I was anything but fine, but athletes did not show pain. Mental or physical. You pushed through. Hit your jumps, smiled at the crowd, and made your coach proud. A tremor ran through me. His worry deepened.

"Okay, yeah, you need to get into the shower." Shaun said, his demeanor switching from cuddle bear to mama bear in the blink of an eye. "Come on." He wiggled free of me, the loss of all that toasty warm Shaun made me shudder. "Get some dry clothes out of the dresser while I get the shower running."

And just like that Nurse Stanton took over. Shaun really should consider some sort of caregiving profession if hockey didn't pan out, which it would, but still, the man was happiest when he was helping others. I sat on the bed, fully clothed right down to my wet socks, and watched him enter the small bathroom linking my room with Jun's. Since Jun had moved out years ago, that room was now Sobo's sewing room, but the shared bath still joined the two.

Shaun was talking away. The taps were turned on. Steam started to creep from the bathroom into my room, yet there I sat like a deflated bullfrog. I had no energy at all. The thought of hauling my ass into the shower was a daunting one, but I knew I had to, so I did.

"Grab something warm," Shaun told me as I moved to slide from the bed. I tested my legs to see if they would hold me up, that was how spent I was. Thankfully, they did, but the thought of Shaun carrying me into the bathroom, then washing my back as I lounged in a bubble bath was a romantic one. Shame there was only a sink, a toilet, and a shower stall in that tiny room.

I pulled out a pink sweater with an anime heroine

on it, some fuzzy leggings, and hand knitted socks. Shaun stood nearby, a solid presence filling me with some reassurance that, if I did faceplant, he would be there to catch me. It was nice to know someone would.

"In you go. I'll see if your mom has some soup she can warm up," Shaun said as I pattered around my room.

I paused at the bathroom door. "No, I don't want any soup. Just… tea maybe. Ask Sobo to make some tea."

He nodded, then reached out to push some lank hair from my brow. "Promise me that you won't purge."

I felt so small standing there. And not simply because Shaun was a moose.

"I won't," I replied in a tiny mousy voice.

"Promise me."

Guess he had some doubts. Given what he had seen once before, that was a wise call on his part. I didn't hold the distrust against him. I was quite the liar when I had to be.

"I promise."

I closed the door in his face with a weak smile meant to ease his mind. Steam billowed around me, the mirror over the sink coated with mist. A good thing. I didn't want to see my face right now. I peeled off my clothes, dropped them into the hamper, and walked past the toilet. There would be none of that. I'd promised Shaun, and I meant it. I'd just have to deal with the million calories I'd ingested somehow. Stepping under the water, I gasped at the shock of the hot pulses striking my chilly skin. After a moment, with my face tipped into the spray, I finally felt the heat begin to thaw me. Now, I sighed at the warmth, greedy for it to soak into my marrow. My movements were sluggish as I shampooed, then soaped up, my thoughts foggy. I knew that I'd fucked up royally, and in front of all the Coyotes. The shame of those guys seeing me sitting in a fucking puddle crying like a baby made me half sick. I swallowed down the rising bile, cranked off the hot and cold, and hurried to towel myself off, my sight never once touching on the porcelain seat.

Shaun was waiting when I left the bathroom, towels lying on the floor, which he insisted on picking up as I crawled onto the bed.

"Sobo is making the tea. She said she knew which one would be the best for you," he called from the bathroom while I wiggled under the bedding. When he exited the bath, I had the blanket under my chin as I lounged against the two bed pillows that someone—

Shaun—had propped up against my headboard. "You look better."

"I didn't even comb my hair," I pointed out as Sobo arrived carrying a tray with some cookies and wearing an aura of serenity. She always knew far too much, it seemed.

"You look better. Drink some of the tea. It is umeboshi plum so will make the stomach upset better," she said in Japanese, her dark eyes skipping to Shaun whom, who she smiled at widely. "You too, have tea, eat the cookies," she said to him in English.

"I will, thank you," Shaun answered softly.

Sobo turned to me. "Your mother and father are not as fooled as you think, Mochi."

I pulled the blanket to my nose so only my eyes and wild hair were visible. "I'm sorry," I whispered into the bedding.

"No need for sorry. Now rest. We will all talk later." She placed the tray on the dresser, gave Shaun a pat on the cheek, then shuffled off, her little slippers making sparks on the carpeting as she went. The door was left open.

"Okay, so plum tea. Never heard of it." Shaun went to the dresser to begin serving tea.

"It's supposed to make your tummy feel better," I said. He nodded as he carried a cup resting on a saucer to me. I released the covers. They slid to my lap as I took the steaming cup. "Thank you. You don't have to—"

"Yeah, I kinda do." He returned to the dresser, returning with his cup on a saucer in one hand and a small plate of rolled butter cookies. "These look like cigars."

"They're called yoku moku. Sobo loves them with tea." Shaun offered me one. I declined. "I think I took in enough sugar for one day. Ilya will be livid when I weigh in tomorrow."

"Fuck Ilya and his obsession with a few pounds," Shaun growled before biting into his cookie with aggression. I wanted to bitch at him, but weak and sick at myself, I blew over my tea instead. Shaun huffed out a weary sigh. "Sorry, I know I promised not to rail on him anymore, but, Kenji, his methods are insane. There is no reason you or the girls should be reduced to this state by your coach."

"You don't know my state is his fault," I protested weakly.

His blue gaze snapped to me from the crumbs on his shirt. "Tell me what happened to upset you so much that you did what you did. Was it someone at school?"

"No," I whispered into my tea. Shaun sat beside

me waiting for some honesty from me. I owed him that. "I got detention for being late to biology. I was too late for group, and Ilya was pissed all the way off about some other coach who got into his business about his students. He ripped me a new one, and I just… couldn't cope. I'm too weak."

"Okay, first off, if Ilya is pissy about an adult coming to him to point out his ancient barbaric methods, then he should mouth off at the adult, not take it out on you. Second, fuck that noise. You are *not* weak. That's Ilya talking that bullshit. You're one of the toughest people that I know."

"Strong men don't binge eat Mounds bars, then break down in a parking lot so completely that their boyfriend has to come rescue them," I muttered into the sweet steam rising from my cup of tea.

"Man, he has skewed your perception of mental health big time," he said around a bite of cookie. "Men are allowed to feel things, Kenji."

"I know."

"No, I don't think you do. I mean, you know in some small space in your brain that is reasonable, but then you listen to Ilya who is toxic AF and his shit poisons your good thinking."

I didn't want to hear all of this. I knew, deep down, what Shaun was saying was right. Ilya was rough on us, too rough at times, but wasn't that what was needed to become a champion? Did guys who broke down over being yelled at ever win the gold? I doubted it.

"Are you mad at me?" he asked.

I glanced up from the tea debris floating in my cup into beautiful blue eyes. "No, I'm not mad at you. I'm just so tired of this all. I think…" I took a sip of tea, then sighed as it coated my dry throat. "I think I'm slipping a little. From the last time?"

Shaun nestled a little closer with care, so as to not spill our tea, but to ensure I felt him at my side. I loved it so much, that strong body of his next to mine. "Like, I had a counselor and everything, but he was… I don't know. He got me through it and all, but I was younger, and now, things are like tripled. School work? Tripled. Skating? Tripled. Life? Tripled. The world? Tripled. And back then, I didn't have sexual shit going on, and it was just…" I took a second to pull my thoughts together. "Sometimes I feel so out of control about everything that I would do *anything* to get some relief. I know this sounds stupid to you, but when I used to purge, it made me feel better. Soothed me somehow."

He bobbed his head, his long legs stretched out in front of him, my feet coming to just below his kneecaps. I loved that he thought he understood, but he didn't. How could he? He'd not been the one with the eating disorder.

"Maybe you should call your old counselor or look into finding one who deals with athletic teens. You could ask your folks to help. They love you so much."

"No, I can't put them through that again. It's not as bad this time," I hurried to say, my sight lifting from my tea to find Shaun staring at me. He didn't seem as if he believed me. "It's not. I just had a little moment, that's all it was. I didn't do anything stupid. I'm not going to make myself sick. I know better. It was just an anxiety attack."

"Okay, if you say so, but will you promise me that, if you feel like you're slipping, will you, please, tell your parents?"

"Yeah, I promise," I replied and meant it. If I felt myself regressing, I would tell my mother or father or even Sobo. I'd reach out.

"Okay then." He looked rather firm for a moment, then the sternness faded to be replaced by something much gentler. "I need to ask you about something you said earlier."

"If it's about Ilya…"

"No, no, it is not about *him*." He spit out the word

him as if it left a taste like moldy cheese on his tongue. "It's about a term you used." His fingers holding the teacup shook as his gaze darted from me to his cup, then back to me. "You used the term 'boyfriend' when you spoke."

Had I? I thought back. Oh. Oh yeah, I had. Shit. I placed my tea on the nightstand to cool while I mentally scurried around like a squirrel searching his tree for a certain nut he could crack open. I needed a nut with a suitable explanation for using such a huge word off the cuff.

"It's not that I object," he hurried to say as I sat there acting like a dipshit who couldn't use his words. "I mean… it's a loaded word, yeah, but I like the sound of it."

He handed his empty teacup to me. I stared down into the leaves in the bottom. "It says here that your friend Kenji also really likes the sound of the word *boyfriend*."

I peeked at him through some hair.

"I didn't know you read tea leaves."

"I'm a man of many talents," I tossed out.

"It has to be secret," Shaun murmured. "I'm sorry, I can't… Being boyfriends has to be secret. My parents don't know that I have feelings for you or anything like that. And then, there's hockey, so that's a whole thing about being queer and out when I hit the draft. Would a team even pick me if they knew I liked guys?"

"I'm sure there are plenty of teams that would love to have you. The Railers are rainbow central. Choo-choo." He snorted. "I made a train sound because they're Railers."

"Yeah, I got the joke."

"What are we like? I mean, honestly, what the hell *are* we?"

"We're boyfriends," he replied, then turned to face me.

"Yeah, we are," I replied as I tipped my face up to meet his lips. The brush of his mouth over mine swept out all the cobwebs that had my thoughts so ensnared. His touch was soft as cotton candy and just as sweet.

The kiss was fleeting, shaky, timid. Perfect.

Just like him.

Chapter Thirteen

Shaun

WE KISSED, LIGHT AND SWEET, AND THEN, I HELD HIM until, at last, I had to go home on. The warmth of Kenji's embrace lingered in my mind long after we parted ways, leaving me feeling buoyant and content. It was one of those rare moments where everything felt right in the world, where worries and fears melted away in the presence of someone you cared deeply about.

As I got a cab to my car, then headed home, I felt lighter, my heart fuller.

Boyfriends.

The roads were quiet, and when I parked on the drive, even if there were elephants walking the sidewalks, I wouldn't have noticed, my mind consumed by thoughts of Kenji. His laughter echoed in my ears, his smile etched into my memory, and the way I'd found him and how he'd turned to me was everything.

Boyfriends.

I walked into the house to the sound of Dad yelling at a west coast hockey game on TV. Normally, his outbursts grated on my nerves and put me on edge, but tonight, they were nothing more than background noise. My mind was still in the clouds, basking in the warmth of Kenji's affection.

Even when Dad's attention turned to me, his words dripping with frustration and disappointment about something else I probably hadn't done, I couldn't bring myself to care. The weight of his expectations felt tiny compared to the happiness I felt with Kenji. For once, dad's disapproval couldn't touch me. I couldn't think about any negatives at all, and I was smiling up until I fell asleep.

My boyfriend.

Only when I woke up to the sound of my alarm did the closet loom large, its walls closing in around me with each moment, and all the happy thoughts were shoved to one side. Kenji was out, and bright, and secure, and I was hidden away. He might want me to be his boyfriend now, but what about when he tried to hold my hand, or just freaking looked at me the wrong way? What then? He deserved more. He deserved what Soren and Felix had, what Jonah and Tyler had, he deserved someone to love him without all the baggage. Then, the dread started, a familiar feeling less about Kenji and how I was going to end up hurting him, and more about facing another day trapped and pretending.

My phone buzzed as I pulled on my Coyotes T-shirt, and I fell on it like a lion on a kill when I saw it was Kenji.

Kenji: Good morning, boyfriend.

Kenji: I can feel you freaking out from here x

Kenji: We can take things slow, just be friends if that's easier for you.

Kenji: Do you want to be friends?

Kenji: Maybe not.

Kenji: I don't want to mess up your life.

I watched as the messages came in, one after the other, and then dancing dots… what else was he going to type? Mess up my life? Was he freaking out as much as me?

I typed a message.

Shaun: Meet me in the locker room in 30 xxxx

I sent a whole load of kisses, just so he'd know everything was okay. The dots danced some more from him, and I could imagine Kenji backspacing and thinking, but by the time I'd left the house, a simple message came through.

Kenji: OK xxxx

Kenji was being so understanding, so supportive. But hearing him talk about waiting for me, it was like a punch to the gut. He shouldn't have to worry about how I felt or wait for me to figure things out. I should have been able to give him what he deserved, but I was stuck in this damn closet. It wasn't fair to him, or to us.

So, what did I do?

I parked the car next to Kenji's Jetta, then jogged into the locker room and burst in like I was some kind of action hero, causing Kenji to jump a mile and clutch his chest. He was already dressed to go out on the ice—this time in a pale pink T-shirt over his leggings, skate guards on, even with his skates on he was still shorter than me. I picked him up and swung him in a circle, hearing his squeak of protest. I held him there, then stepped back until his skates were on the low bench, which made us closer in height.

"Hey, boyfriend," I whispered.

He locked his hands behind my neck and gave me the sweetest smile. "Hey back," he said and wrinkled his nose, which was so cute I slipped one of my hands up to cradle his cheek, thumbing at his cheek bone, and then, stole a soft kiss.

He sighed into the kiss, and I traced his lips with the tip of my tongue, just wanting more of a taste, and the sigh became a cautious touch of his tongue to me. I'd kissed girls before, hurried, darting tongues, and the overwhelming scent of perfume, but this was different. All I could smell was shower gel, and Kenji, and the ice beyond the doors. Perfect. It was on him to deepen the kiss—I hadn't seen him with a boyfriend, and maybe he needed to go slow, or maybe he'd had boys kiss him, and this was nothing new.

My boyfriend.

He tangled his hands in my hair, and pressed against me, his kiss so sweet, his hold on me strong, and then, we were kissing as though we didn't need to breathe. For ages we stood there, wrapped around each other, and the taste of him was intoxicating. A loud bang beyond the locker rooms was enough to startle us apart, and he was smiling, his lips damp, and his eyes half closed.

"Good morning," he whispered as I helped him down off the bench. He tugged his T-shirt down, no room in those pants to hide anything, then sent me a smile. "Boyfriend."

I grinned at him, not caring that I was going to be late out on the ice and the bang had been my dad arriving, and fuck, the shit I'd be in…

"Have a good practice, boyfriend," I murmured back.

"You too."

He almost made it to the door. "Kenji?" I called, and he glanced over his shoulder.

"Yeah?"

"Land those jumps for me?"

He winked then. "Always."

I dressed for the ice, and by the time I was out there, Kenji was working on jumps and Dad was red-faced and pacing up our end. As soon as he saw me, he went dead still, and as I skated over to him, I felt the anger even before he began to speak, and I set about starting my stretches. Practice was tough, the worst so far, probably due to my late night and Dad's constant haranguing, and it was worse when Kenji left the ice, Ilya close behind, leaving me all on my own with Dad.

"You're slow!"

I pushed harder, but Dad didn't stop.

"That fairy beat you out on the ice! That's dedication, and he's doing a girl's sport, hell, it's not even a sport, and he still beat you out here!" He said for my ears only and pointed at Kenji. "Twirly Girl was practicing while you were still tying up your damn skates."

I stiffened. "What did you say?" I asked.

He acted as if I were asking him to repeat himself. "Twirly Girl over there—"

"No." I snapped. I couldn't take it anymore. The constant scrutiny, the overbearing presence—it was suffocating. I turned to him, my voice trembling with frustration, and fuck, was I going to cry?

"Who do you think you're talking to?"

"Stop!" I yelled; my words laced with defiance.

His eyebrows furrowed as he struggled to

maintain his composure. I didn't answer back, I was all about keeping things on the level, ignoring the man who wanted me to achieve what he hadn't been able to. I was done. I was suffocating with it.

"Excuse me?" Dad's knuckles turned white as he clenched his fists, his temper simmering just below the surface. But I was done today—just done with tiptoeing around him.

I squared my shoulders, meeting Dad's gaze head-on. "I don't want you here in the mornings with me anymore," I declared, the words tumbling out before I could stop them. "You're a bigoted, misogynistic, hateful loser, and I don't want you here!"

Dad's expression darkened, and I knew he was this close to jumping the barrier and... god knows what he'd do, because I'd never pushed back. I'd never felt as if I deserved to be something other than someone who owed his dad for the early mornings, and for buying my kit, but something had changed in his hatred of what Kenji was.

Twirly girl. Nothing. No one.

"Get off the ice!" Dad roared, and I slid back at the power of it, knowing Kenji and Ilya would have heard that.

Something in me broke. "You don't get to call Kenji anything derogatory again."

"I'll call *it* what I want."

That was the moment I snapped. I could feel the ice under my skates, and the hardness in my belly, but I couldn't stop.

"No." I skated up to the barrier. He could reach me if he wanted. He could lean over and hurt me, but it would be the first time he laid hands on me, and the last, and I was done with his hateful words.

Kenji's friendship meant something to me, and I needed to be honest with myself and own my truth. I had to before it destroyed me, and what I wanted with Kenji. This was for holding his hand, for kissing him, for shuffling up next to him at the noodle shop and holding him close. This was for friendship that had nearly been broken, and for all the things I'd kept quiet.

"Leave Kenji alone."

"That fairy, Jesus, next thing I know you'll be wrapping your stick in pride tape—"

"I'm bisexual!" The words hung heavy in the air, tension crackling between us like electricity. I braced myself for his reaction, unsure of what to expect, but not surprised when he reared back from me, anger replaced by shock as if I'd knifed him in the chest. His face twisted into a mask of fury and disbelief. His eyes narrowed; his lips pressed into a thin line as if my words had somehow offended him. "I'm queer." It seemed as if that part needed repeating.

His reaction was immediate and visceral. "No son of mine is bi- anything, pick a side, girls, and stay there," he spat, his words dripping with contempt. It felt like a slap in the face, the rejection stinging more than I had anticipated. What did I expect? Hugs all around and undying love?

I stood there, rooted to the spot, feeling the weight of his words crushing me. It was as if my entire world had shifted in an instant.

I refused to cower before him. "This is who I am, Dad, I'm just like Kenji. I'm queer, and I'm coming out, and if that means I lose out on the NHL, well that was your dream, and I'm sick of fighting for it." My voice trembled. "I can't change that, and I won't apologize for it."

There was a moment of silence, the tension between us thick and suffocating. And then, without another word, my dad turned and walked away, leaving me alone with my thoughts and the harsh reality of my truth. I leaned over the boards, my stick caught between my legs, alone in the rink, the crash of the doors the only indication that Dad had ever been there.

Mom. I needed to call Mom.

"Sweetheart? Shouldn't you be in class?"

"Mom…"

"Shaun? Sweetheart? Is everything okay?"

"I told Dad, and maybe he's coming home. Don't be there, okay?"

She made a soft sound of distress, but it wasn't because of me. "He won't take it out on me," she lied. "Anyway, I'm at the mall with Aunty June. How about we come to you?"

"Please."

"We'll be there in twenty."

"Okay."

I skated back to the locker room, showered, dressed in my uniform, then ended up sitting on a bench under a wide maple tree where Mom would see me. I'd thrown my future career into disarray, I'd challenged Dad, and the next call I made was to my agent, with Leo answering on the third ring.

"Hey, Shaun?"

"Leo, I'm bisexual, and I like a boy," I blurted because even coming out to Dad hadn't made it any easier to say.

I could see any path to the NHL vanishing, but what did I want more? Did I want to live with this secret chipping away at me. How long would I need to hide for? When I was maybe drafted, could I have come out after that? Or what about when I was five years in, ten, when I retired? What would Kenji be doing all this time? Waiting?

"Thank you for telling me," Leo said without hesitation. "Are you okay?"

"Yes." And I *was* okay. I was fine. I was seventeen, and I'd known forever that I was a different person inside, all hidden away, and yeah, I was more than fine. I felt fizzing in my body, and a weight as big as a tank lifted from my shoulders.

"Good. Now, this is fine, Shaun; you have me on your side. Are you somewhere safe?"

"Safe?" Did he mean my dad, or did he think I was going to do something stupid? "Dad isn't here, and I'm happy. I'm good."

Leo seemed relieved. "Your identity is yours and yours alone. I'm so proud of you, Shaun, and here's what I can do to help you…"

By the time Mom picked me up Leo had reassured me that if I wanted to chase the NHL, he was one hundred percent in my corner. He also had college prospectuses in line, and an assurance that he could figure things out with the NCAA if I wanted to go down the college route—I was good enough to get a scholarship, he said, and maybe that was what I wanted? I didn't know, but he said he'd help.

I thought about sending Kenji a simple message, but something stopped me. I didn't want him to think I'd come out for him, but that was what he *would* think, and then, he'd always worry I'd turn away from him.

I needed some time to show him what he meant to me.

I needed some time to be me.

Then, none of that delaying made any sense at all. I scrolled to our conversation and stared at the empty space for me to type, and I didn't know what to say. This seemed like a moment I needed to remember, but I needed to explain everything leading up to what had happened. We didn't have any classes together today, but I wouldn't be in school—I couldn't face school, I needed my mom to be safe—but he'd worry if he didn't see me. Right?

In the end it was the easiest thing to type.

SHAUN: *NOT TO MAKE A BIG THING OF IT, BUT I JUST came out to my dad, and he was pissed, but Mom is heading out to get me.*

Shaun: *I'm okay.*

Shaun: *Mom's okay.*

Shaun: *I'm out. I'm OUT.*

Shaun: *We can hold hands.*
Shaun: *xxxx*

HE WOULDN'T REPLY NOW, GIVEN HE WAS HALFWAY through his class, but he'd see it as soon as he was out. I scrolled my phone and found a photo of us that I'd taken to get printed—the last one of us before our friendship had broken apart. Us smiling—him in silver and black, me in a hockey jersey, heads close together with goofy smiles. Why did I think it was okay to give up our friendship?

Then, I opened Insta and posted the photo, along with hearts, and a simple tag *#boyfriends #ProudToBeMe*

By the time Mom arrived, Aunty June right behind her, I was on adrenaline overload, and I fell into her arms. She hugged me so hard I couldn't breathe, and I think I was crying. Or laughing. I couldn't tell.

My name is Shaun Stanton, and I'm bisexual.

Chapter Fourteen

Kenji

IT WAS BEYOND FREAKING AMAZING TO BE SEATED AT the ice rink on the Chesterford campus as Shaun's official boyfriend.

We'd even hugged it out before the game in the parking lot. His mom, my folks, and the entire student body saw us. And no one said a word. Maybe some gave us dirty looks, but not a single smear or hateful comment was heard. Of course, his dad and my coach weren't in attendance, so that probably helped. Shaun and his father weren't communicating at all, which was stressful beyond belief. His texts, from the moment he had come out to now—five days after the

Stanton men had blown up at each other—were always bright, but with an undertone of sadness.

I'd known his house wasn't all sunshine and kitten whiskers, whose was? But the announcement of Shaun's bisexuality had put an enormous strain on an already tense household. That first night after the showdown with his father, Shaun had confided that he suspected his coming-out might be the cause of his parents separating. I'd told him no, that wasn't in any way the cause.

Things had gotten so bad that his mother had asked his dad to move out. I wasn't sure what was going to happen next for them. Whether they would divorce, or reconcile, or do counseling was up in the air, but whatever went down, Shaun was an innocent caught up in all that mess.

If his folks split, it was on them. He was only a kid. They were the adults, and it was their marriage. Deep down I sort of felt that his dad leaving might be a good thing for everyone.

We'd talked until two in the morning that night. He had so much to get off his chest, the words pouring out of him in text after text. At last, when I nodded off during a discussion about junior prom, we both decided to get some sleep. The next morning, we met on campus, hugged, kissed, and walked into school hand in hand.

And now, I was squished between my mom and Jonah, Tyler's boyfriend, as he snapped pictures of the game taking place down on the ice. The Coyotes were beating the stuffing out of the team from Hershey.

Shaun was great as always. The whispers about him being bi had spread like wildfire through the school. We didn't do a thing to quell the talk. We held hands, hugged, kissed, and did everything else all the other couples on campus did. Shaun seemed so much more comfortable in his skin now. And on the ice as well. I grinned back at his mom, sitting behind us, after Shaun stole the puck from a Hershey forward to take a prime shot on goal. He didn't score, that time, but he was on fire all the same.

After the second intermission, the Coyotes had a commanding lead of 5–0, and the Hershey goalie was at his wits' end. Soren and Tyler teamed up on a speedy breakaway, passing back and forth as they streaked down the ice to the Hershey net. The away goalie had no chance. He moved left to try to defend the net against Soren. Soren shuttled the puck to Tyler. The Hershey goalie could not get back fast enough to block the sneaky little shot Tyler took. The score was now 6–0, and the Chesterford fans were delirious. My throat was sore from cheering. It was at times like this that I wondered if I had made the right call to switch. Figure skating was amazing, and I did enjoy it, but it was a solo sport. At least for me. I spent all my time with Ilya. My parents knew little of what went on behind the scenes with my coach. I kept all the crummy stuff to myself because they were paying Ilya a lot of money to coach me. His agreeing to take me on had been huge. There was no way I was going to tell them that he made me feel anxious at times, or that he said off-color or hateful things about everyone who wasn't Russian.

They'd be so hurt. So, to avoid hurting them, I only let them in on the good things. No mention of the ugliness or the weigh-ins or the crushing need to maintain weight. And no way in hell was I telling them about the parking lot incident or the hourly urge to find a scale to step on. They'd been through that with me before, and it had nearly killed them with worry. I wasn't about to burden them with my stupid shit again. It was under control. Life was good. Great even. I had a boyfriend who stood by me. A group of friends. A loving family.

So, what if I had a grumpy coach? I could handle it. I *could* handle it.

I shook off the worry to see that Shaun was making a move on the Hershey goalie that I'd never seen him make before. He skated behind the net, the puck in front of him. With a flick of his wrist, he picked the puck up on the blade of his stick, snuck around the side of the crease, and flipped it in. A Coyote goal. Un-freaking-believable! We all shot to our feet to cheer as the score ticked up to a mighty 7–0 with the Coyotes in control.

After the game, we all met in the parking lot, the boosters heading to the Hot Pot Noodle Shop to grab tables for a ramen celebration. Shaun walked out with a wet head and a smile just for me. I ran to him, threw myself at him, and hugged him as hard as I could.

"You are amazing!" I whispered into his ear before kissing his earlobe.

"That goal was for you. Because I know you're going to Michigan soon for the Snowflake competition."

I drew back enough to stare into those beautiful sapphire eyes of his. "You are the best boyfriend in the entire history of boyfriends."

"Nah, that would be you."

I kissed his face until he got giddy, then shifted me around to ride on his back. All the way to the noodle shop with the rest of the team and families coming behind us. I held on tight, the cold wind biting at my face as we marched along. I was so happy. So incredibly, stupidly, happy. And so incredibly, stupidly, sappily in love with the guy carrying me as if I were a leaf on his strong back.

THE MORNING OF THE SNOWFLAKE CLASSIC ARRIVED in Michigan with a bitter blast of air off Lake Erie that made the hairs in my nose freeze as I jogged to the rink sitting right along said body of churning water. The waves slammed into the shore as Ilya and I slowed to catch our breath. Yeah, he was still in that good a shape. The sun was still trying to carve its way through the thick storm clouds that had the great lake so chaotic. We'd been up since four a.m. to ensure that we got a run and a final bit of practice time in before the competition began at two in the afternoon. My weigh-in today had been good. I'd come in a pound lighter after doing some intense fasting yesterday. Breakfast today—after practice, so I wasn't sluggish—would be something light. Ilya nudged me. We picked up the run. The rink at the hosting university felt warm in comparison to the brutal winds outside.

I changed after a cooldown spent with Ilya going

over the routines for my programs. Once I was in skating gear, I hit the ice. There were two other skaters present, a couples duo I knew from making the rounds of the eastern competition circuit. Ilya was also on the ice, so going over to talk to the couple was not going to happen.

"Give me that," Ilya said, his cheeks still red from the run. I handed him my ice bag, a small tote that held all my warm-up goodies like tissues, a bottle of water, notes for my routine, lip balm, anything I might need so I didn't have to leave the ice during practice. Ilya hated interrupting a practice for a tissue. "Now, we will go over the short, then the long routines."

"Okay," I said, then skated off to warm up with a lap of stretching and swizzles, working out the kinks before heading into some easy Russian stroking followed by crossovers. Then, I moved into step sequences. Ilya watching distractedly as he also worked on notes. When I felt warm and loose, we would begin churning things out a bit more. This was when Ilya would follow me on the ice, shouting at me to push, feel the music, push, spring off your toes, push, let me see a certain move one more time. One more time. One more time. Push. Arms up. Bend and extend. Push. Why are your crossovers like preliminary skater? Push. Get up. Do it again. Push. Push. Push.

An hour later, I came off the ice, exhausted, lightheaded, and in need of a shower and some deodorant.

"We will have breakfast at the hotel in one hour," Ilya told me as he handed me my practice bag. I dug into it looking for a hairband, but none were to be found. "One hour. Do not be late."

"No, I won't. I promise." We left, the wind roaring now, the cold scouring my cheeks, leaving my wet hair to freeze. Wasn't spring supposed to be here by now? The hotel was a mile away, and we ran back. When I hit the lobby my hamstrings were screaming.

Over by the breakfast buffet, I spied Trent Hanson with several of his skaters. They were laughing as they piled their plates full of food. My stomach snarled to remind me it was empty. I'd grab an apple later. Trent glanced up, saw me, and smiled. I returned the smile, then started over to say hi.

"You have no need to speak with that man," Ilya snapped, grabbing me by the arm. He herded me into the elevator, away from the other skaters stirring around in the lobby with their coaches at their sides. "You have no need to talk with any of them," he informed me as the elevator doors closed with a soft *ping.* "This is not a friendship rally. This is a competition."

"It's not a best friend race," I mumbled and got a strange look from my coach. "Someone said that on an episode of RuPaul once."

"Ah, the transvestite. That your parents allow you to watch such things saddens me. If I had a son, I would not allow him to view such perversion. Americans are too lax."

I sighed so hard I felt wobbly. Yep, we were all sickos over here. The doors couldn't open fast enough to suit me. Of late, every minute I spent with Ilya felt like a lifetime. He'd always been gruff and demanding. Intense. But ever since I had come out as pan, his bias had begun to creep into our time together, and it really was starting to work its way under my skin. I thought about speaking up, but knew if I did, he'd probably scratch me just to show who was in charge. Or maybe not, since I was the only one of his students who had gotten his permission to attend. The skater girls had been heartbroken when he'd told them. They'd left the ice sobbing. He'd told them to work harder instead of consoling them. There were times I despised Ilya so much.

"Maybe it's not wrong to accept people for who they are," I muttered as we reached our floor. His gaze—stormy as the lake—flew to me. I tipped my chin higher, exiting the elevator as soon as the doors whooshed open. "I'll meet you for breakfast."

He followed me out of the elevator, mumbling in Russian about who knew what. I stalked to my room, scanned the key, and stepped inside. My legs barely carried me to my bed. Collapsing into the hard mattress, I had a moment of sheer joy. I'd snapped back at Ilya. I rolled to my back, wiggled out of my coat, and dug my phone from my practice bag. Ilya did not allow cell phones during practice, or competitions, or in his general presence. My attention was to be on him and him alone.

Tons of notifications rolled in after I turned the Android on. My folks were on the way, Jun was going to meet them here, sans the girl he'd brought to the art show. Shame, because she had been nice, pretty, and able to put up with his happy horseshit as Dad liked to say. Shaun, along with the guys from the Coyotes—Soren, Felix, Tyler, Jonah, and a few others, were also on the way having left super early. The drive from Harrisburg to Detroit was eight hours. Pretty considerable. That the guys were willing to put that much time behind the wheel, and then cough up cash for a hotel room overnight, said a lot about my friends. My family kind of had to come for the allotted days I'd be skating. Today was short programs, tomorrow long, and the closing day was exhibition skates for those who could afford to miss school. Since most were homeschooled, it wasn't a problem, but for me, I had to be absent for that day. Mom and Dad were cool with it though.

I caught up on social media, sent Shaun a selfie of me with puckered lips that I added hearts and tiny lips to, as well as a message to drive safely. I told him I missed my boyfriend and could not wait to kiss him in real life.

He hit me back with a line of red hearts and a quick shot of him and the guys standing beside Soren's dad's SUV. Grandpa Rowe was the chosen driver as he was retired and thought a road trip with the boys was *pretty groovy*. His words, not mine. Grandpa Rowe was also along because there were limits on how many kids could be in a car with a driver under the age of eighteen in our state.

Smiling at the ceiling after talking with Shaun, I sat up, fought off another round of dizziness, and got into the shower with care. The hot water revived me a little. By the time I was seated across from Ilya in the hotel eatery, I felt better, less wrung out, more alert.

Ilya was eating eggs, bacon, and some fried potatoes with some coffee on the side. I made a slow crawl around the breakfast buffet. Everything was fattening or loaded with sugar. Bagels and muffins. I opted to pick at a nectarine and sip at a cup of unsweetened green tea.

"Do not overeat or you will be sluggish," Ilya commented, then began informing me of the scores I'd need to progress to the Eastern High School Regionals at the end of the month. I'd have to do well here, or I'd miss out. I'd come into this competition with some good scores, but there were some real tough competitors skating today. "I think you are going to do fine if you remember to hit your jumps."

I rolled my eyes as I picked at my nectarine. Like, no shit. Did he think I didn't want to land my jumps? Why did coaches say such dumb things?

I ate half the nectarine as Ilya reminded me of everything that was on the line. How his reputation was now resting on my shoulders, since the girls had disappointed him. Awesome. No pressure there or anything. My tea made my tummy warm. The nectarine half did its job. The rumbling had stopped, so I could now focus on skating.

We went to his room after breakfast, watched tapes for an hour, and then, it was finally time to gather up our gear and head to the rink. This time we took a taxi. I enjoyed my last chance to check my texts and was thrilled to see that Shaun and the guys had arrived safely.

My nerves were starting to ramp up as we made our way to the men's locker room. Ilya was like a mastiff at my side, protecting me from the media with a stiff arm, leading me past other skaters, and directing me to my seat in the locker room.

He was a meticulous man. He inspected every facet of my outfit from the neck of my black and green sequined top to the toes of my skates. He made me polish my skates again to ensure the judges knew I kept them in good condition. He did my hair, applied what little makeup he allowed me to wear, then left me alone for a bit to deliver the CDs of my music to the sound engineers at the rink. Two copies in case something happened to one set. As I said, Ilya was nothing if not thorough. I glanced around at the other kids here, most my age, and their coaches. I smiled at them, then placed some earbuds in to try to counter the anxiety bubbling away in my gut.

I was fully into the latest cut from Beyoncé when someone sat down beside me. My gaze flew to Trent Hanson, all bundled up in a thick yellow parka, his eyes lined, his lips painted bright pink, and his hair swirled up into a hairdo Effie Trinket would envy.

"Hi there," he said as soon as I yanked the buds

out of my ears. "I know you're getting into your zone, and I totally respect that. I just wanted to touch base with you. How are things?"

"Good, things are really good."

"And Ilya is treating you well?" he asked, his gaze flicking around the locker room as if looking for someone. Probably my coach. Ilya didn't like Trent, and I got the vibes the feeling was mutual.

"Yeah, he's great," I lied and got a nod from Trent.

"Okay, good, good. You still have my card?"

"Yeah," I said. It was in my wallet. Tucked behind my driver's license and the lone condom I carried just in case my boyfriend and I ever went that far. Neither of us were in any hurry.

"Good. If you ever decide to change your outlook on how you wish to proceed in skating, just know that I'm going to be opening a school in Harrisburg. This traveling every weekend to see my husband is not cutting it, so, if you ever want to chill with my gang or me or check things out, give me a call."

"Oh cool, sure, yeah. I'll do that."

He smiled widely. "Excellent. Good luck."

I watched him return to his skaters, confused about the impromptu visit. That rarely happened because Ilya forbade people from talking to me before a competition.

As the time ticked down to my time on the ice, I began to feel queasy and unsettled. The nectarine was acidic in my stomach, giving me some killer heartburn. I was sweaty as I rose to my skates for warmups. The rink was filling up, fans and family hooting as we made our way to the ice. I handed Ilya my skate guards, took a sip of water and skated out. The ice swam a little bit, the sounds of the other skaters and people in the stands seemed grating. Loud. Just too loud. I ran through my warmup, my costume soaked through already, my vision doing this funky kind of psychedelic sixties shit.

"I don't feel right," I told Ilya an hour later as my time on the ice neared. I'd been fighting through the nausea, but now, I was having trouble recalling what my short routine was. Shit.

"It is nerves." He adjusted my collar one final time as the rink announcer began my introductions. "Focus now. Do not let the little things break your concentration. Remember to smile at the judges. Do not let your attention waver. When you feel as if you cannot give more to the routine, that is when you must push yourself to give more."

I half heard what he said, the sound of my name

blurred in my ears. Ilya shoved me to the ice, my hand automatically coming up in a small wave. The crowd was muted, the lights far too bright, my hands clammy. I made it to the center of the ice, unable to recall how this routine began. Panic set in. My music filled the rink. I heard my father shouting my name. Or was I hearing things? I pushed off to start my routine, the footwork sloppy as I struggled to remember what came next. Unable to recall, my thoughts sluggish, I made a round of the ice, tears welling, and did the only thing that I could remember knowing how to do that Ilya would be happy with. I launched into the first jump of my short routine far earlier than it was scheduled, my speed lacking. The salchow was an utter disaster. I didn't push off my toe pick properly. The jump collapsed in on itself just as the lights, sounds, and smells of the rink flickered once, twice, and then, blackness as the ice raced at me.

Chapter Fifteen

Shaun

EVERYTHING SLOWED DOWN.

One moment, I'd been in my seat, excited and nervous as Kenji glided onto the ice. His movements were a little jerky and strained, and at first, I wondered if something wasn't right, but then, it was probably just nerves. When the music started, Kenji was a beat behind, and I'd seen him practice this— even on his worst days, he was never a beat behind.

"Something's wrong," I blurted, but no one was listening as the music swelled. My chest tightened with worry, breath catching in my throat. I couldn't shake the feeling of impending doom, a sense that something was about to go bad.

And then, Kenji's steps stuttered, he managed to collect himself for a jump, out of synch with the music, and then, he fell, and the crowd gasped.

Before Kenji hit the ice, I was on my feet, adrenaline propelling me forward. I scrambled over Soren and Felix, their hands reaching out to catch me as I caught myself in them in my haste.

People were talking, shouting.

Is he moving? Is he dead?

Everyone was talking at me, over me. I think I heard Soren call my name, but they were a distant hum as my focus narrowed on Kenji. I jumped the last few steps, vaulting the boards, close to ending up on my ass, and I went into a crouch to stop myself sliding. Paramedics were already skating out to Kenji, crumpled like a ragdoll in the center of the rink, his arms splayed, his cheek flat to the ice, his eyes closed. I slid my way over, and by the time I was there, he was blocked from me by paramedics as they assessed his condition checking his pulse and vitals.

The crowd was silent, and I realized that the music had stopped.

"Blunt trauma to left temporal region. I have a pulse," one of them said, his tone clipped and professional, and it nearly cut me off at the knees.

There was blood. He'd fallen hard, skidding as his head bounced off the ice, his face scraped raw.

"Get back!" one of the paramedics snapped at me.

I stared at him, not realizing he was talking to me or how close I'd moved. I was getting in the way, and horrified, I stumbled back.

"Kenji…"

Someone took my arm, tugged me further back., Ilya was there, someone shoving at him—Soren? Felix?—so who had my arm? I glanced up. Dieter, the former Railers winger, gripped me tight, and it was his husband, Trent, the figure skater, shoving Ilya, pushing him back from Kenji.

"He'll be okay," Dieter reassured me as I tried to get free. "Let them work. They have him."

There was a backboard, the paramedics working, other officials forming a circle around Kenji, blocking people from seeing him.

Blocking me.

"I need to…"

"I know, kid, I know," Dieter murmured, and tugged me a little further back as there was a flurry of motion. My stomach churned with fear as I watched everyone work on my boyfriend. Finally, they had Kenji on a backboard, his neck supported—he wasn't moving—then onto the stretcher. I wanted to reach out to Kenji, to reassure him that everything would be okay, but I was rooted to the spot, unable to move. All I could do was stand there, my eyes locked on him, willing him to wake up.

"Kenji!" I called, trying to wriggle free, but Dieter was strong, and I was useless to do anything but stand in place. We followed the stretcher in a line, Trent pushing Ilya to one side as we entered the kiss and cry area where Kenji's mom and dad were waiting. His mom was crying, his dad as white as a sheet, his brother Jun grief-stricken. Then, the entire group of us stopped as the ambulance pulled away.

"Our car is in VIP parking," Dieter said. "We'll take you to the hospital." He was talking to Kenji's parents, but Mrs. Kelly took my hand.

"Please. The four of us." She glanced up at me and nodded, asking me if that was what I wanted.

"Thank you," I said.

More tears coursed down her cheeks. "He will want his boyfriend with him," she said.

Dieter's car screeched to a halt in front of us.

Soren's grandpa hovered with the rest of our group. "We'll follow," he said.

A surge of panic washed over me as Kenji's parents and I clambered into the back of Dieter and Trent's car. This wasn't how today was supposed to end. Kenji was supposed to fly, and win battles, and go home, just like any other time on the ice.

He *had* to be okay.

We headed to the hospital, but there was no sign of the ambulance as we hurried down busy streets.

"I'll kill Ilya," Trent said under his breath, but I could hear because I was in the middle leaning forward, watching for any sign we'd catch up to Kenji. Even though Dieter was driving, he was reassuring his husband, either that or he was calming him down.

"You can't kill him, babe."

"I swear, if that kid…"

"I know," Dieter replied, although Trent hadn't finished the sentence.

If that kid… what? I went blank. Dies? No, he hit his head. Panic gripped me, my chest tight.

"No!" I snapped.

Trent wriggled in his seat to stare at me. "It will be okay. He'll likely have a concussion, but it was a clean fall." He squeezed my hand because it was the only one he could reach, but he was talking to all of us.

"What about the blood. There was blood," Kenji's mom said.

"Head wounds bleed, so it makes it look worse, Mrs. Kelly. He'll be okay."

As soon as the car stopped, we all piled out, but then, it was standing and waiting and sitting on hard chairs, and more waiting, until a doctor finally came out for Kenji's parents. That left Trent and Dieter down one end of the seats, and Jun slumped in a chair staring into a cup of cold coffee way down at the other end, with my friends and I in the middle of them. Ilya was on his phone, talking loudly in fast Russian.

"What if it's serious?" I asked no one, but Soren nudged my elbow. He'd been quiet, texting his dads and holding up his phone every so often, for what reason I didn't know. Maybe to get a signal. I couldn't look at my phone, not when the screen would open to the photo of me and Kenji.

The door opened and Kenji's parents walked out, and I was up and at their side in an instant. "Is he okay? Can I see him?" I asked in a tumble of words, as everyone else crowded behind me.

"He's dehydrated, his sugar levels are…" Mrs. Kelly placed a hand over her mouth, "he hasn't been eating, or drinking, he's… he has stitches, and a concussion, they have him on a drip to…" She sobbed then, and Mr. Kelly took her into his arms.

"Can I see him?" I asked again, but no one was listening.

My stomach twisted as I heard about Kenji's lack of eating and drinking. It felt like a punch to the gut, a heavy weight settling on my chest. Worry, guilt, and frustration swirled inside me. Worry for Kenji's health and well-being, guilt for not realizing the extent of his struggles sooner, and frustration at the situation we found ourselves in. It was a horrific reminder of how fragile and vulnerable Kenji was, and I couldn't help but feel overwhelmed by the enormity of it all.

"He will be okay," Ilya patted her arm, "sacrifice leads to reward."

Mr. Kelly held his wife tight as she lurched at Ilya. "What did you do!" she shouted at him.

He stepped back, held up his hand. "Nothing that any other coach wouldn't do," he said, as if he was shocked she'd asked.

Then Soren was there, holding out his phone. "I recorded what Ilya was saying, and… okay, Stan, tell them what he said."

Stan? A familiar voice filled the room with heavily accented Russian—Stan, the Railers' goalie, who'd once played with Soren's dad.

"Hello is all," he began. "Ilya asshole explain to friend he not playing at making champion, and people to… what is word… listen hard and do what he says. Too heavy skater means no flying. Say Kenji too heavy, tell him limit eating, thinking to add drug to drink like others. Says Kenji is waste of space, and Ilya might give up and going back to Mother Russia before big people in charge catch him up. He is bad man," Stan paused. "To fix this, I know people," he added ominously.

Ilya went pale and took a step away from us. Trent evaded Dieter and shoved Ilya back against the wall, but Dieter levered his tiny whirlwind of a husband off, just to replace him, pinning Kenji's coach flat.

"Shoving people around was my job, and I remember how to do it, babe," Dieter deadpanned. "Thanks, Stan," he called to his former teammate.

"I know people," Stan repeated, and then, Soren held the phone to his ear and backed away. Security headed over to us—there was shouting, there was cursing, and Ilya was escorted from the premises—as was Dieter, who laughed the entire time.

I slumped to the chair, Trent next to me, his hand on my knee, and we waited, until people went home, and it left only me, Kenji's parents, Jun, and Trent.

"He's asking to see you," Mrs. Kelly said to me

after they and his brother were allowed in and had spent an hour in with him.

I walked into the hospital room, my heart heavy with worry and guilt. Kenji lay there, pale, hooked up to a drip, a bandage on his temple over the stitches. He started apologizing, his voice weak and filled with regret.

"I promised I was okay, and I wasn't. I know you'll hate me, but I wanted to say, I want to do better, but I can't do it on my own, but it's all too much, and…"

His words trailed off, and my heart ached at the sight of him, so helpless and defeated. I wanted to reassure him, to tell him it was okay, but the words caught in my throat. Instead, I pressed a kiss to his forehead, smoothing back his hair, then reached out and took his free hand in mine, offering what little comfort I could.

"It's okay, Kenji," I whispered, my voice barely above a murmur. "You're not alone. You have me."

But even as I spoke the words, doubt gnawed at me. Could I help him? Would he be okay with only me and his family in his corner? Was Trent being here something that would help Kenji or hinder him—did Kenji want the former Olympic skater anywhere near him?

"I'm sorry… I'm sorry… please don't hate me," Kenji kept repeating, and I reassured him that everything was going to be okay.

"I could never hate you."

"You came out for me, and I ruined everything."

"I came out for me," I told him for the third time in a row. "You'll be okay."

Only, I didn't know that at all.

Kenji was allowed to go home after two nights in the hospital, with strict care instructions, and I was still in town, with Trent having paid for my hotel room, clearing everything with my mom so I could stay. I was determined to be in the car with Kenji going back home.

The last person who visited Kenji was a man called Lukash, a friend of Trent's, former figure skater, and now, a Clinical Psychologist specializing in eating disorders. When he knocked on the door to visit with Kenji, despite Kenji pleading with me to stay, I had to leave.

Kenji needed help from an expert.

He didn't need me.

TRENT DROVE ME HOME THE MORNING THAT KENJI was released, and we talked about hockey, about the

Railers, about his husband, about the weather, but nothing about Kenji, which made for a long road trip. I had my earphones in pretending to listen to music but was actually tracking down every podcast I could find on figure skating and eating disorders, and every scrap of information I could find on Ilya. When we were an hour from home, I realized that this might be the only time that I could ask Trent questions.

"What can I do?" I asked.

Trent threw me a glance. "Be a friend," Trent said.

"What will happen to Ilya?"

Trent glanced in the mirror and indicated, pulling into a McDonalds, and encouraging me inside.

"Talking needs food and coffee," he said, but he wasn't angry, he smiled at me and seemed thoughtful. I *was* hungry—ravenous—and Trent piled a ton of food on me and joined in with some of it.

"As to Ilya," he began. "I've made an official complaint. It's up to Kenji whether he wants to support that complaint, although a couple of the other students he taught are willing to go on record." He sipped his coffee, thoughtful, staring out of the window, his jaw tense. "Ilya gave one of his girls slimming pills, encouraged her to vomit to stay at weight, and she's been interviewed with her parents."

"So even if Kenji isn't well enough to go on record, there's someone else…"

"Yes. We have enough for revocation of his coaching credentials, possibly a criminal case." Trent was frustrated, and his lips thinned, so different from the endless smiles he typically gave to the world. "I'll fight this the whole way. I'll make things different."

I nodded along as Trent detailed plans about cleaning house and making things safe for young figure skaters.

I listened and hoped what hurt Kenji wouldn't happen to anyone else.

And I worried again that I would never be enough to help Kenji.

That maybe I'd lose him.

And that hurt.

Chapter Sixteen

Kenji

I WASN'T SURE WHAT HURT WORSE: THE CONCUSSION or the first family-based therapy session with Dr. L, or Artem Lukash Ph.D. as he was officially known. Dr. L had a long silver beard, sparkling blue eyes, and tiny glasses sitting on the end of a flat nose. Dr. L insisted on being called Dr. L, his Ukrainian accent subtle, now, after many years of living in the US treating teens with eating disorders. It seemed that Lukash had been a figure skater when he was younger and had struggled with body image issues himself. He explained that, back then, there was little known about such things and far less talked about. Which was fucking tragic.

I'd been home for a week, the concussion still an issue. I couldn't stand quickly, and the sun made my head ache. The knot on my head had gone down, and the scrapes on my face were now scabs that looked fucking terrible. I had draped a towel over the mirror in my bathroom, so I didn't have to see my face. The face of a loser.

Dr. L opened the session with "So, today I would like to talk about the towel over your mirror." I threw a glower at my older brother; Jun shrugged. "Does it make you angry that Jun reported that to me?"

"Yeah, because he needs to just go back to college and pretend I'm not even alive the way he has for years," I snapped, irate at the betrayal. As soon as the words were out of my mouth, and I saw the hurt in Jun's dark eyes, I felt terrible. Guilt. More guilt. So much guilt and shame bubbling inside me made me feel ill all the time. "I'm sorry."

Dr. L leaned up to hand me a box of tissues. Great. We'd not been here ten minutes, and I was on the verge of tears. I was so weak.

"There is no need to be sorry about what you feel, Kenji," Dr. L said as I yanked a few tissues free from the yellow box, then wadded them into a tight ball. "Jun, do you understand why Kenji might feel betrayed betrayal?"

"Yes, I do, but I'm done seeing things, then pretending they're not a problem. We all saw Kenji behaving in odd ways, limiting his food intake, and yet, we all said nothing."

Mom and Dad spoke up. Mom in tears, Dad citing that they had noticed nothing. Then, he started to tear up.

"We should have noticed," Dad coughed, his eyes welling. "We should have paid more attention to you, Kenji. What kind of parents allow this to happen to their child, twice?"

All four of us started talking at once, reassuring the others it wasn't their fault. Dr. L sat back, stroking his beard with one hand, jotting down notes in an old spiral-bound notebook with a puppy on the front with the other.

"Okay, let's all take a moment to recenter," Dr. L broke in when I began crying silently into my ball of tissues. "It seems to me that everyone feels as if they could have prevented Kenji from sliding back into unhealthy eating habits, but in reality, there are more factors at work here than busy family members who turn a blind eye to a potential problem."

"His coach is a prick," Dad snarled, his anger a living thing.

Dr. L sat back and let my father empty his spleen

about Ilya. I had nothing to add. I'd been bullied by an adult whom I'd looked up to for a long time. Mom sat beside Jun, her cheeks wet, her beautiful gaze on me as Dad ran out of ire. For the time being anyway.

The silence in the doctor's office was deafening.

"I'm sorry," Dad murmured. "I know anger isn't helping anything, but I just want to pummel that man for what he's been doing to our kid."

"I let him do it, Dad," I piped up to break the silence. I stared at the small plant on the light wooden coffee table, the roots visible through the glass pot. Behind me a tabletop waterfall ran, the sound of the water soothing, I guessed. Jun frowned. "No, I did. I mean… yeah, I knew he was being overly strict. I lied to everyone to cover up for him." I glanced from my brother to my counselor. "Why did I do that?"

Dr. L seemed to be pondering that question. "Perhaps, that is a query for you to work on for our personal sessions, Kenji." Ugh, yeah, here we go. "I will say that it is very easy for a young adult to be manipulated by an adult in a position of power to do things to help shield the abusive adult from discovery."

I sat back, stunned at the word abusive. Throughout my entire time under Ilya, I had never thought of his methods as abusive. Super strict, ridiculously outdated, but abusive? No, that word had never entered my mind. Maybe it should have…

"What can we do now, Dr. L?" Mom asked as Jun shifted uncomfortably in his chair. That he had decided to take a leave from his studies to be here for therapy still amazed me. And it made me feel loved. The amount of attention and care that had been showered on me over the past several days made me cry on the hour. All my friends and the staff from Chesterford, the student body, the skater girls, the Coyotes, and a ton of my fellow figure skaters. Cards, flowers, texts, personal messages, well wishes, just about anything a person could send via the internet had rained down on me like a warm spring shower of support.

And then there was Shaun. My boyfriend. He was my pillar of strength.

He was at my house every day after practice until eleven. Sometimes, we simply napped. Sometimes, we did homework. I had no clue when I would be going back to school, so I was doing my work online, or trying to. The concussion made things rough, and I would need to stop every ten minutes or so to give my eyes a rest. Shaun would feed me cookies or bring me tea from Sobo or rub my temples. Sometimes, we would just lie on my bed, cuddled close, and talk.

I shared more with him than I probably ever would with anyone else. Aside from Dr. L with whom, who I knew I was going to have to come clean, if I ever wanted to resolve my eating disorder.

The rest of the hour was less intense, but just as tearful. Dr. L explained his process, that he was available to me twenty-four hours a day via text or phone, and that his outpatient skills coaching involved several key components we would work on as a family. He was very set on family involvement at all levels of my recovery. We touched on group therapy with fellow adolescents under his care. We discussed field trips that the teen group would be taking to grocery stores, restaurants, cooking classes, meal planning, and a slew of other things designed to help us learn healthy eating habits that would carry us to and into adulthood.

There were a ton of discussions ahead of me in the teen group, as well as in family and personal sessions. Things like being aware of the influence of social media, mindfulness, anxiety management, and medication for depression and anxiety. He suggested I start on antidepressants for a multitude of reasons, and I agreed, as did my parents.

"Will I be able to skate on meds?" I enquired as my brother reached out to grab my hand. Out of nowhere. I threaded my fingers into his. It had been a long, long time since he'd shown me any kind of physical affection. Jun just wasn't that type of guy. Unlike Shaun, who was all about the hugs.

"I'm going to ask you to refrain from skating for a few months, Kenji. Sometimes, adjusting to new meds can be tricky. Also, since so much of your disorder centers on skating, I think we need to let that stressor go until we have you on more solid ground. Do you feel okay with that?"

I nodded. Yeah, that was okay. "Sure, yeah," I said, feeling a lightening of pressure on my shoulders that I hadn't been aware of carrying.

We all rose when the doctor did, shook hands, and went out into the waiting room to schedule about eight million sessions. My life for the next few months was going to be nothing but group therapy, family therapy, solo therapy, school—as soon as I got cleared by my medical doctor—and field trips with a bunch of other teenagers with body issues.

Thank all the gods for Shaun.

"Do you want to stop somewhere for lunch?" Dad asked as we rode down from the fourth floor of the medical building. The March winds were meek today. Seemed the month was going out like a lamb. Warmer weather and spring buds sounded really good. I looked up at my father. "Oh. Should I not do that? Should I not mention eating out?"

"No, hey, it's cool. I'd like to maybe get a milkshake after I get my prescription filled," I said, giving my father a little smile.

"Let's get a vanilla for you and a chocolate for me, then mix them half-and-half like we used to do when we were kids," Jun suggested, shrugging into his jacket as we exited the elevator.

He was tall like Dad, but with my mother's delicate facial features. I was all Mom right down to my small feet and emotional way of dealing with the world. She loved to hug me tight and call me her fellow creative. She with paints on canvas, and me on the ice. Only, not on the ice for a long time now maybe. I wasn't sure how I felt about that. Just another thing to figure out.

"Yeah, okay, let's do that," I replied, my hands in the front pockets of Shaun's letterman jacket. It was far too big on me, but I loved that about it. And him. My phone buzzed in my back pocket, and I smiled. That would be my boyfriend texting me during gym class to see how therapy session number one of a billion went. If he got caught on the phone, Mr. Limon would make him do fifty laps of the gym.

I'd tell him it went fine. Then, I would show him my half-and-half milkshake.

TEN DAYS LATER, I WAS SITTING BESIDE SHAUN IN HIS car, parked in the student lot, chewing on my lower lip. The doctors had given me the all-clear to return to school with the proviso that, if I started experiencing headaches from staring at screens or the blackboard, I was to go to the nurse's office to rest for a bit.

"You okay?" Shaun asked, turning off the engine, but leaving the playlist running. "You can take another day. Your folks will be totally fine with you staying home a little longer."

"No, I'm… I need to get out of the house."

That was no lie. My family loved me to bits, I knew that, but they hovered. Sobo had made me so much tea and baked me so many cookies that I was unable to look at a tea pot without burping plum. Mom was all about healthy eating, and we did some meal planning together, which was nice, but she tended to watch every bite I took, then smiled at me for chewing and swallowing. Dad was all about the veggies, leaping into the mix to toss salads every night, then tell me about his days in the Air Force and how performance was related to the fuel you took in.

As if I were an F-15. Also, very cool that he cared, but I wasn't a jet. I was a confused kid with body image issues.

Jun was the only one who didn't flutter around me like a damned neurotic hummingbird. Jun was actually pretty cool. I'd forgotten how much fun he could be when he let himself just chill.

"Okay, sure, I get that," Shaun replied, his voice pulling me out of the light fog I felt I'd moved into all the time. The meds were kicking in now, and they helped with impulse control and my anxiety. "No one will say anything about you, Kenji."

"I know." I didn't know at all. I felt vulnerable. A skinny Asian-American kid in a stupid uniform with scabs on his face like a leper whom the world saw fall on his face at a major competition because he had an eating disorder. Yep. Like that wasn't giggle fodder for the masses. The stigma about eating issues was strong, and for guys who suffered, it was even worse, as eating issues were feminized. "I just wish I hadn't been so stupid that day."

"Hey, you weren't stupid." He took my hand in his bigger one, lifting it from where it rested on my thigh. I looked from the kids filing into classes to find his blue eyes on me. He kissed my bruised knuckles. "You fell and hit your head. Happens in hockey all the time. No one made fun of Tennant Rowe when he had his head injury."

"That's different."

"No, it is not. A concussion is a concussion."

"And my other issues?"

"Are mental health issues that you're getting help with. There are all kinds of athletes who are taking time to deal with their mental health. It's not a dark secret anymore. You're so strong, Kenji, I wish I could help you see that about yourself."

I leaned over the console that held our takeout hot cocoa cups to kiss him on the mouth. A good kiss, one with lots of passion because he inspired me to love, not only him, but myself.

"Wow," he whispered when we parted, his lips bright pink and slick. "That was…" He reached down to push at his crotch with the heel of his hand. "I need a minute here before we go inside."

"Me too," I teased, shifting in my seat to alleviate the boner in my slacks. Dress pants did nothing to hide the darn thing. I sat back down. We sipped our cocoas as our dicks deflated, and then, we exited the car. Shaun came around to clasp my hand. We'd made it nearly to the front door when I realized I'd left my backpack in the car. Ugh, man, my head was muzzy. After running to get my backpack, I met Shaun at the front doors. Soren, Felix, Jonah, and Tyler were sitting on the steps just inside the foyer, smiling at me as I approached them.

"There he is," Soren called, making me blush as other eyes swung from lockers and conversations to me. "Dude, those scabs on your face look cool. Like you got into a bar fight with some rowdy biker guys."

"Yep, that's totally the story that I'm going with. Bar fight with biker dudes. They lost. I won."

Felix laughed as he offered me a fist to bump. Jonah started jabbering at me about an interview with the school paper about my incident on the ice.

"I'm not sure," I replied with honesty, taking, and using one of the things I had learned in group therapy last night. Saying 'no' is okay.

"He's not ready for that kind of thing yet," Shaun said, his tone kind, but firm.

Jonah stumbled over an apology.

"No, man, don't be sorry. It's cool. Maybe someday, yeah?" I said. He nodded, then peeled off to go to class, Tyler at his side. Soren and Felix also left, leaving us to make our way down the emptying halls. I was nervous as I neared homeroom.

"I wish I could stay with you all day," Shaun whispered as we stood in the corridor, facing each other.

"Like a big beautiful golden retriever psychiatric service dog."

He blushed the prettiest shade of red. "Woof," he said softly, stole a kiss, and then, watched me enter homeroom, closing the door behind me. I could feel the stares of my fellow students.

"Welcome back, Mr. Kelly. If you take your seat, we can do roll call," Ms. Porter said, her smile warm as the spring sun shining in the windows. I nodded and sat down, then glanced at the door. There stood Shaun, waving at me through the tall, narrow window in the door. I wiggled my fingers back at him. He blew me a kiss, then took off just as second bell rang. Yep, he was going to be late to class, no doubt in my mind.

"Hey, Kenji, I saw your fall, then heard people saying you had mental health stuff going on. I take anxiety meds too." Laura Kerston turned at her desk to confide in me.

"Yeah, me too. I have since freshman year," Lance Kilroy told me across the aisle.

"Thanks," I said to the other kids who had reached out to me. Kids I didn't hang out with or spend much time with, but who shared a thing with me. "I totally forgot my backpack in the car this morning. Is that normal?"

Laura told me about her first time on meds and how she had left the trunk of her car open, with all the groceries she had bought for her mom, sitting in student parking for twelve hours. Lance relayed a funny story about how, when he'd first gotten on his meds, he'd slept all day at a picnic table in his backyard until his folks had come home and discovered him sprawled out under the oak tree. They had a picnic that night.

I laughed with them. And they with me. Maybe this was going to be okay after all…

Chapter Seventeen

Shaun

THE ONE PERSON I DIDN'T EXPECT AT THE BREAKFAST table was Dad, but there he was, in all his glory, perched on a stool, Mom sitting opposite.

"Morning, Shaun" he said, his hands laced on the counter, an unfinished mug of coffee to one side.

"Dad," I acknowledged, then chose a stool next to Mom, my elbow touching hers. I couldn't help but notice the weary look on my dad's face; his eyes were bloodshot, and there were dark circles beneath them. "What are you doing here?"

He hesitated for a moment, but it was clear he had something important to say, and my stomach twisted with apprehension.

"What is he even doing here?" I asked Mom instead.

She reached for my hand and squeezed it. "He wants to talk," she said.

I faced Dad. He winced at whatever he saw in my expression, and I braced myself for whatever was about to come.

"Shaun," he began, his voice hoarse with emotion. "I've… been doing a lot of thinking since I left," he said, his gaze fixed on the table.

"Since Mom kicked you out, you mean."

His eyes brightened. "I love your mom."

"Funny way of showing it," I groused, and Mom squeezed my hand again.

Dad cleared his throat. "I messed things up. Not just with you, but with your mom too. Too much anger, too much…" He scrubbed his eyes. "All I could see were the things I'd lost, instead of what I had. I love you both so much, and the pressure in my head overshadowed everything. I'm sorry. I've been stupid."

I listened in stunned silence as my dad opened up about his own insecurities and failures. He spoke of the pressure he'd put on me to succeed, his own dreams of making it to the NHL. He admitted to being pushy, even bullying at times, and how he'd driven a wedge between us with his anger and aggression.

"When your mom told me to leave, she insisted I go to therapy," he confessed, his voice barely above a whisper, then he let out a soft laugh. "'For anger management', she said to me. Only that just made me angry, for God's sake. I told myself I didn't need therapy, that I needed to get back some of the pride I'd lost and that you were the stop on that journey. But I went, and I was ready to argue my way out of a paper bag, only that was the point wasn't it. I was lost in it, and I'm not saying I'm fixed, or that I'm moving home. It's just one step, but I'm trying, Shaun. I want to do better. For you, for your mom, for our family."

I felt a lump form in my throat as I listened to my dad's heartfelt apology. It was clear he was showing remorse for the pain he'd caused, and for the first time in a long time, I allowed myself to feel a glimmer of hope that maybe he could just be my dad?

"Mom?" I asked.

She leaned her shoulder against mine. "Go on, Ed," she encouraged Dad.

"I want to apologize to you, Shaun," Dad said, meeting my gaze head-on. "For everything. I know I've let you down, but I want to make things right. And I understand if you don't forgive me, but I'm willing to do whatever it takes to earn back your trust. I'll support you whatever you want to do—NHL, college, or even not playing at all. It was my dream to lift the cup, get the money, the plaudits, not yours, and I pushed you too much."

I could see the sincerity in his eyes, and despite everything, a part of me wanted to believe he meant what he said. I knew it wouldn't be easy to rebuild our relationship, but perhaps it was worth a shot.

"Thank you, Dad," I said, feeling some of the weight of resentment and hurt lift from my shoulders. "I appreciate you saying that, and I'm trying to see that you mean it. One thing though; I'm bisexual, do you understand that? If I ever have any kind of career, in hockey or not, that is who I will be forever, and I won't hide it. It's never going to change. I have a boyfriend, Kenji…"

"I know."

"And?"

"I know I'm wrong. I love you. *All* of you, all the little bits, the hockey, the history nerd bits, the jokes we used to tell each other, the way you trusted me when I taught you how to ride a bike. Please, Shaun, tell me I haven't completely fucked up?"

"And you won't quit the group, and you won't make Mom cry?" *Or me.*

"I will never stop going to group. I will try my hardest to never make your mom cry again, and one day... maybe we'll be together again?" He was talking to my mom, but he had a long road to prove he was a good man, and I would defend my mom to my dying breath. Hashtag dramatic.

"If Mom is willing to give you a chance, then I am too."

A flicker of relief crossed my dad's face, and for the first time in a long time, I allowed myself to believe that maybe, just maybe, there was hope for us yet. When he left, it was after we'd hugged, and after he'd held my mom's hand and thanked her over and over.

"You think he's changed? Just like that?" I asked her as we watched him leave.

She sighed. "Not yet, but maybe, one day he will. He's still the man I love, still your dad. So, I want to try. Do you?"

I pulled her close and hugged her.

"Yeah."

I LEANED BACK AGAINST THE WALL OUTSIDE THE biology lab waiting for Kenji so I could tell him about the talk with Dad, and then, walk him to lunch and, yes, that was me, wanting a glimpse of my boyfriend and maybe to steal a kiss.

"What are you doing out here?" Kenji asked as he and Tyler exited the classroom.

I tugged him to me and kissed him, then hugged him.

"Missed you," I murmured, and he snuggled into me, and I never wanted to move.

"Laters," Tyler smirked and ducked around him into the crowd of students heading to the cafeteria. We'd stopped going there for food, making our own picnic anywhere we could find space, where it was okay for Kenji to relax, then try his hardest to eat. He never minded that I wolfed down the equivalent of two people's food, and today would be no different. We found a space under the back stairs, laying out my coat and sitting cross-legged next to each other as I polished off my lunch, and he picked at some grapes.

"Dad was at our house this morning."

Kenji shot me a glance. "Are you okay?"

"Sure, yeah, he's going to a group, anger management or something."

"He's not a bad guy," Kenji said.

I snorted a laugh. "If you'd heard some of the things he said about you—"

"I did. I heard a lot, but you know, he was scared

you'd end up like him, and I don't mean that in a bad way. I mean that he's so poisoned with disappointment, and he was angry all the time, for himself and for you maybe ending up as disappointed as he was. God, does that make any sense?"

"Strangely, it does."

"And he's not naturally evil like Ilya."

I shuddered at that thought. He'd gone back to wherever he was from, but he wouldn't be coaching in the US, or indeed, a whole slew of countries, any time soon.

"We need to go on a date," I blurted. "A real one, just me and you."

"Not the noodle place," Kenji said, then dipped his head, focusing on the last remaining grape in the bowl.

"No, better than that," I decided and went through my list of places to eat where I could take Kenji. In fact, my mind raced so hard with ideas for our date, I never realized how quiet he was.

"Can we not just do this?" he asked after a while. "I like it here, just you and me, with no one watching."

"Of course, but… I want to romance you."

He leaned against my shoulder, and I wrapped an arm around him. "This is romance for me. Just us." He repeated that last bit, and something in his words pierced my stupid heart. Kenji had been through so much, and I wanted a date that would show the world how much I liked him, wanted to make sure things were perfect for him, but every date idea I had revolved around food in some way, and what Kenji was saying was that he just wanted it to be us, but also saying *no eating in public.*

Movies? No, popcorn and candy are staples, and I didn't want to trigger any discomfort for Kenji. Dinner out? Definitely not, too much focus on food, and I knew how stressful that could be for him. Maybe a picnic? No, that was even worse, with all the snacks and sandwiches.

I sighed in frustration. Kenji deserved a great date, something that showed him how much I cared and supported him in his recovery journey.

"Are you okay? Did I say something wrong?" Kenji asked.

"God no, I was just… it's a pop quiz thing," I lied, and thankfully, he didn't push me for any more. What kind of date could I do that didn't mean we'd be putting eating at the middle of things?

Then, it hit me like a bolt of lightning. Our shared love of history? Maybe we could spend the day exploring a museum or visiting a historical site. That way, we could focus on learning and experiencing something new together, without any pressure around food. Perfect!

A smile spread across my face as I envisioned us walking hand in hand through the exhibits, sharing interesting facts and stories with each other. It wasn't about the food; it was about the connection we shared and the memories we'd create together.

"And now you're grinning like an idiot."

"We're going into Harrisburg on Saturday. I'll pick you up at eight. We're not eating anywhere, food isn't an issue, but wear sneakers and a smile. And clothes of course."

He closed the lid on the empty grape container. "Shaun?"

"Yep?" I was lost in planning the perfect historical day, the Civil War Museum was first on my list, and maybe, when we were out there, we could talk about what was next for both of us. Leo's suggestions about possible futures were still playing on my mind. Did I want what Dad wanted for me? What he'd sacrificed so much for me to do? Or did I follow the college path? Did I want to leave Mom now? Or Kenji? Or did I want to stay and be a normal kid for once? Would I miss hockey more than anything if I didn't push to get out there?

"Is it too soon to think maybe, possibly, I could be going past best friends again and straight on to love?"

My brain froze. What? I never expected it to be him to say it first! I've wanted to tell him that for so long but didn't want to push. He took my hesitation as an answer, tugged himself away, forcing the grape box into his backpack.

"It's okay," he said, in a small voice. "Maybe, one day, if I'm fixed, I can—"

I grasped his arm and tugged him onto my lap, so he was straddling me, and then, cradled his face.

"You don't need fixing. It's you, me, *us*. Always," I said, my words tripping over themselves. "And I don't *think* I love you; I *know* I do."

He ducked his head, a flush of scarlet on his cheeks, as he stared into my eyes. "That's good," he said.

"So good."

⸻

As Kenji and I walked through the National Civil War Museum, I couldn't help but feel a sense of awe at the history surrounding us, and I knew Kenji felt the same way. The exhibits were filled with artifacts and information about one of the most pivotal periods in American history.

Kenji, ever the history buff, was practically bouncing with excitement as we discussed various artifacts and shared interesting facts about the Civil War. His passion for history matched mine, but the way he talked about things was contagious, and I found myself hanging onto his every word as we wandered through the museum, hand in hand.

"I can't believe the Battle of Gettysburg lasted for only three days?!" Kenji asked, his eyes lighting up with enthusiasm. "It was the turning point of the war, and it seems like it should have lasted forever."

We paused in front of a display of Civil War-era weapons, and Kenji launched into an animated explanation of their uses and significance, which was an area of history I didn't know much about. I listened intently, soaking up every detail and feeling grateful to be sharing this experience with him, and all the time that I was listening, I was falling more in love.

As we moved through the museum, stealing kisses whenever we thought no one could see us, I couldn't shake the feeling of contentment that washed over me. Being with Kenji felt right, like we were meant to be together, and every smile he threw my way was this gift I wanted to hold close.

Eventually, we made our way back to the entrance, both exhausted, but happy. Before heading home, we decided to take a detour to a nearby overlook to enjoy the view of the city lights below. Or rather, I decided, because I didn't want the day to end.

Sitting in my car, the warmth of Kenji's hand in mine, I couldn't resist pulling him closer for a kiss. Our lips met in a sweet, lingering touch, and for a moment, the rest of the world faded away, and then, one kiss turned to two, which became more.

I could kiss Kenji forever.

Each time we parted, breathless and smiling, it was to share a secret in the dark. Kenji's fear of what he'd done, and how he was going to be, and what his future could be; me with my fears of my own future and all the decisions I had to make.

He glanced up at me with a glint of excitement in his eyes. "I've actually been thinking," he said. "I don't want figure skating anymore, not where I let it hurt me."

"I get that."

"I want to go to college to study history. My sobo has money put aside, and I know I won't have the scholarship chances, but it could be enough if I get a job and stay close so I can live at home."

I felt a surge of pride and admiration for him. "That's amazing, Kenji," I said, squeezing his hand.

"What about you?"

Me? I had no idea.

No wait, I *did* have an idea, or at least a vague hope.

"I'm not going in for the draft. I want to go to college, and if the NHL happens, it happens."

Wow—I hadn't said that out loud to anyone. As soon as the words left my mouth, I began to spin impossible dreams. What if we went to the same college? What if we could get a place together—me on a scholarship studying history, him being with me —sharing classes, sharing a life. Probably impossible, and I was sure there would be a ton of rules about where a student lived in the first year, but…

"What if I tried for a scholarship to Penn State? It's a D1 college, and I'm sure it has an amazing history program."

"I know it does," Kenji murmured. "It's on my list."

My heart leaped. "I could study history, you know I love that, and I can play hockey, and we could end up living together and have this whole life ahead of us."

"It's good to dream," Kenji said, but he didn't sound sad—if anything his voice held excitement at the potential.

"If…" I didn't want to voice the possibilities, and he seemed to get that.

"If is a very powerful word."

"Something to work toward?" I asked with hope.

He leaned over and kissed me. "Definitely."

Chapter Eighteen

Kenji

It was weird how easily I could get up and out of bed when I knew I was going to be spending time with Shaun.

When I'd been meeting with Ilya at the ass crack of dawn, I'd hated it. Through a long talk with Dr. L a few weeks ago, I had worked out that it wasn't the act of waking up and practicing I disliked so much, it was knowing I had to face Ilya and his unrealistic goals. It seemed so clear now that I was distanced from him. What a pity that the skater girls and I hadn't seen it when we were living it. Dr. L said that was something that was experienced by many an abusive relationship, especially young adults who had no skills in dealing with such unhealthy situations. Sitting at the rink on the Chesterford campus with a cup of hot chocolate and a skinny bagel with whipped cream cheese, I felt good. Gifts from Shaun for accompanying him. He'd also given me a few dozen kisses along the way. I liked the kisses way more than that bagel, but I was eating it. Slowly. Bite by bite.

Deep down, where the half a bagel sat in my belly, I felt as if I should be out there at the other end of the ice. I felt guilty for abandoning figure skating. The sport hadn't done anything to me; my coach had. Yet, I couldn't imagine lacing skates on my feet now. Whenever I did, I got clammy, and my pulse rocketed. Just another thing to hold against Ilya.

"Hello, fellow early bird," I heard as Trent Hanson made his way to me, his smile bright, his eyeshadow a brilliant blue that went well with the coat he wore. He carried a thermos of coffee, as well as a bag stuffed with all the things a coach might need for his students. The bag was quilted and pink as his cheeks. Over his shoulder hung a pair of well-loved black figure skates. "Mind if I sit?"

"Please do," I replied, lifting a few cloth shopping bags from the seat beside me. "Let me move these."

"Thanks. Oh boy, this weather huh? Yesterday, it was forty, and today, they're calling for it to jump into the sixties. Spring in Pennsylvania." He settled into his seat, placing his bag and skates on the floor beside his tiny feet while juggling his coffee.

"Yeah, it's unpredictable," I offered, then glanced at Shaun, working on his stick-handling.

"He's very good," Trent commented after a moment or two of silently admiring my boyfriend's skill. "Dieter says he has a real chance of making the pros."

"He will. I know it." I replied proudly.

"I'm sure he will. So, Kenji, while we have a few minutes alone, I have a couple of things I want to talk to you about."

I peeked over at him, my bagel resting on my thigh, half-eaten. I was pacing myself. If I stuffed too much in at once, I felt anxious. Little steps, little bites. It was my new motto.

"Okay," I said hesitantly before lifting my cup to my lips.

"Are you here to skate?"

"Oh. No, no, I'm not… I'm not ready for that."

He nodded, a shank of deep purple hair falling into his eye. He blew it away with a puff. The man changed hair colors like I did my nail polish.

"Totally understandable. I have a few of my new

students showing up today for an introductory class. They used to be in your group."

Oh, the girls. Anita, Evelyn, and Harper. "Cool, they're good skaters."

"They requested me and, of course, I couldn't deny them. The school was gracious enough to let us use the ice here. Are you okay with seeing them skate?"

I nodded instantly, then shook my head, then exhaled. "Sorry, I don't know? I mean… I want to say yes to make you happy, but Dr. L says that isn't healthy. That I need to learn how to speak up to authority figures politely, but firmly so…"

"I understand one hundred percent. Thank you for being honest. That's why I wanted to speak with you before they showed up. They're due in thirty minutes."

"Okay, thanks. Shaun and I will be gone by then. We're going to Whole Foods to pick up foods for our two-month anniversary dinner tonight. He's cooking for me. It's all stupid romantic."

"Oh, my gods, that is delightful! Congrats, babe!" He gave my knee a squeeze. "I'll be quick about things then, so as not to make you late. Okay, so I have a confession to make and a story to share with you. One that might make you hate me."

"I doubt it." That was impossible. Trent was too much of a friend for me to ever get mad at him. He'd been nothing but supportive and—

"I was the coach who spoke to Ilya about you." Oh. Oh. That news hit like a punch to the face. It blindsided me. "I know, it was none of my business, but in a way it was. I've known Ilya for a long time. His methods are outdated, to put it nicely, and dangerous to put it bluntly. A child should never leave the ice in tears. *Ever*. We're not here to punish our students or bully them. We're here to guide, to coach, to teach. Teaching should not involve tears."

I didn't know what to say, so I said nothing yet. The hurt was strong. Ilya had been terrible to me after someone—and now I knew it was Trent—had called him out on his strong-arm bullshit. I'd suffered because of Trent interfering.

"If you're mad," Trent said with caution. "That's totally reasonable. I just wanted you to know that the reason I approached him was out of concern for your health. I could see the unspoken signs of his mental abuse on your sweet face." He stared out at the ice. "I had a friend way back—one of Ilya's first students. She was a bright and brilliant quasar of a girl. Her skating skills were way above mine at that age. We skated at the same rink in Pittsburgh, where Ilya had first settled after coming to America to live and coach. I watched her slowly wither. The bloom gone from her cheeks, the sunshine leaving her eyes, and the weight slowly slipping from her slim frame. She left skating when she became too weak to compete. My friend... she never skated again. She passed at seventeen from her eating disorder."

"I'm sorry," I choked out, tears blurring my vision.

Trent dashed at his eyes, his hands quaking, as the memory clawed at him. "I am too. She was a beautiful, vibrant flower crushed by an evil man who should be *nowhere* near young, impressionable minds. So, when I saw some of the same patterns showing up with his treatment of you... I had to speak up. I should have done so earlier, and for that I apologize. Perhaps, I could have spared you some pain."

I had no clue what to say in the face of his agony and mine. The urge to apologize for something—everything—was strong, but I held back from doing that. I'd done nothing wrong. Still, I felt empathy for his past, for his friend, and for him.

"I'm really sad that you lost your friend," I replied cautiously, wishing I knew what to say next. "I guess they didn't know much about eating disorders back then."

"Well, things were getting better, but still lacking. Much like today in some regards, but at least we are making progress with understanding mental health issues. Movie stars, top athletes, famous singers are all taking time to deal with their mental health. And that is a good thing!" I nodded, then dared a glance at him. His gaze was still on the ice. "Pity someone didn't speak up for my friend back then, but they didn't know the warning signs. I do." He stared right at me. "I know them well, and so I spoke up. Perhaps that was the wrong call, but I couldn't let it go without saying something. I'm pretty mouthy. Just ask Dieter."

That made me smile a little. "I wish I was mouthier."

"Oh. You'll grow into it, trust me. Give yourself ten or fifteen years, and you'll be up in a bitch's face just like a drag queen." He snapped his fingers, then popped his tongue.

"I'm not mad at you," I said after the sound of a puck hitting the glass faded off. Shaun mouthed *sorry* at us, then resumed shooting at the net.

"You take some time to decide that. I hope you're not, but you're certainly entitled to be upset with me."

"No, I'm sure. I'm not mad. Thank you. For caring enough to face his wrath."

"Anytime, dumpling. Can I give you a quick hug?"

"Sure."

We embraced carefully, as I had a bagel on my lap, and he was holding a thermos of coffee.

"Okay, phew. I'm all verklempt. I'm going to go touch up my face. Thank you for being so precious, Kenji. And if you ever decide to come back to our sport, call me. I will always have an opening for you."

"Thanks."

Trent patted my shoulder, gathered his belongings, and left me alone with my cold bagel and lukewarm cocoa.

The bagel half was still resting on my lap when Shaun joined me fifteen minutes after Trent's departure. Trent was now on the other side of the ice, reading over something as he waited for his students.

"Hey," Shaun said, hockey stick in hand, duffel bag with his gear over his left shoulder, his cheeks bright red from cold and exertion.

"Hey." I puckered. He bent down to kiss me. His lips were cold.

"So, that looked like a pretty serious conversation with Trent. Everything okay?"

"Yeah, it's okay." It wasn't great. I was conflicted emotionally but knew that I could talk it out with Dr.

L Monday after school. That would help me untie the knots Trent's confession had tied up in my chest. Okay seemed like a fitting word. I wasn't mad at the man. Maybe I was mad at Ilya the most for taking out his anger on me instead of speaking his piece to Trent.

"All right then," he said as I handed him the bagel half, then rose. "You sure you don't want this?" He always asked that when I passed food to him. I assumed it was his roundabout way of trying to nudge me into maybe taking another bite without coming right out and asking me to eat more. We were both learning. I nodded. He took two bites, and it was gone. My eyes flared.

"Mockey mabe me mungry," he said around a mouthful of cold bagel.

"Dork," I teased, rose to my toes, and planted a kiss on his cheek. "Let's go." I held out my hand, and he took it, his grip soft, but firm. Perfect.

THE GROCERY STORE WAS EMPTY.

We had been waiting outside for it to open, so we had the place to ourselves, aside from the employees.

"Okay, so what are we looking for?" I asked as we

walked through the fresh fruits section, Shaun pushing the cart through the international produce area. "Oh cool, look at this! They have Hokusai. We should find good ingredients for a hot pot. How does that sound?" I picked it up, then showed Shaun, the oblong-shaped head of Chinese cabbage.

"Yeah, cool. Do you like hot pot?" I nodded and got a bright smile. "Then, I'll make you a hot pot you'll never forget."

"This is much more fun than shopping with Dr. L and the group," I said as I placed the cabbage in his cart. "I mean, I get that it's good to learn what to buy for healthy meal prep and all that, but sometimes a man just wants a doughnut, right?"

"If we bought a doughnut, would you eat it?"

"Probably not," I admitted. Shaun gave me that hangdog look that tore me up. "I'm sorry, but I *am* trying."

"Hey, no, do not apologize. You're doing great. Maybe we could share a doughnut for dessert unless you have something in mind that's more traditional to go with hot pot?"

"Hmm." I walked along, tapping my chin. A worker moved past, pulling a trolley filled with cases of vegetables. "I'm not much of a cook or baker."

"Me either, but they have a wide variety of

international foods. Let's take a spin through the bakery section before we leave?"

I bobbed my head. Sweets were a problem for me. I knew half a doughnut, or a muffin top wouldn't add ten pounds, but I was so conditioned to avoid even the crumbs that enjoying a cookie or tart made me anxious. I hated my brain. I longed to be just like the other kids who could swallow junk food down like an anaconda. No lie, I had watched Soren polish off a six-pack of cupcakes in less than three minutes the other day. And all he did afterward was burp and smile with his lips coated in bright yellow frosting.

"Hey, you okay?"

I shook off the envy. "Yep, fine. Just thinking about Soren slamming down those cupcakes at lunch the other day."

Shaun snorted in amusement. "Soren has a thing for his grandma's baking."

"Obviously. So, *maybe* we can check out the baked goods. Maybe they'll have something that's not so huge and loaded with sugar."

"This is America. Everything is huge and loaded with sugar."

Yeah, true enough. We took our time, choosing some of the healthiest things we could find for our hot pot. We loaded up on the fresh veggies. Besides the cabbage, I tossed in some chrysanthemum greens, yu choy, lotus root, winter squash, fresh mushrooms, and a package of frozen beef meatballs. Into the cart went a burner, a divided hot pot, and a skimmer. A package of chopsticks, some mushroom soup base, and a jar of peppercorn mix to add to the broth. There was a package of sliced ribeye, as well as a deli platter of shrimp. We added some glass noodles, as well, for the starch, and then, visited the bakery department.

"Oh hey, how about this?" Shaun asked, holding up a container holding a fish-shaped cake.

"That's Taiyaki," I explained, rushing over to check out the treat in his hand. "Sobo has the pan for this but hasn't made one in forever. It's really good. It's filled with red bean paste and is all warm."

"Oh cool. Do you want to get it, then, for dessert?"

My thoughts began to wonder—how many calories were in the cake? What about when it was combined with the hot pot meal? Would I feel out of control?

"You can just nibble on the tail," Shaun whispered to me, his words a soft puff of love and caring that helped ease the wave of control loss. "I can put it back, Kenji."

"No, don't. I want to nibble its tail. I just need a

second." I felt like a fucking idiot standing in the bakery department as I worked to recall my mindfulness exercises. Breathe in, breathe out, let the anxiety flow away with each exhalation.

Oh hey, hi there anxiety. Thanks for letting me know that I've faced and dealt with a lot today. A fish cake is totally okay. I've got this. Eating small meals is good for me. We can let those worrisome thoughts go now.

Shaun stood at my side, his hand on my lower back, his presence comforting as I worked through the moment. I opened my eyes, looked back over my shoulder, and saw him there beside me.

"You are the strongest person I have ever known," he whispered, stole a chaste kiss, and held the fish cake in the air as if asking if it went into the cart or back on the shelf.

"I'd like some fish cake, please," I whispered just for his ears.

"This is going to be the best two-month anniversary hot pot meal in the history of two-month anniversary hot pot meals."

I was pretty sure he was one thousand percent right.

Epilogue

Shaun

JUNIOR PROM WAS THE BEST OF NIGHTS AND THE worst. The best of it was that I got to go with Kenji, and I hadn't had to ask him, it was simply happening.

Because he was my boyfriend, and we were together.

The worst of it was wearing this suit, which I swore was trying to burst at the seams, having Mom popping her head around the corner of my door to check on me, Dad sending me an awkward text telling me to have fun, and both Soren and Felix sitting on my bed.

Yep, that was the worst bit, and not because of Soren, but because Felix was an idiot.

"Your muscles have muscles, future-NHL-Star-Shaun," he deadpanned, and Soren elbowed him.

"I've been lifting because I have the… whatever," I ended when Felix smirked and fell back on my bed. Why am I even telling them again? Leo had organized some guys from Penn State to watch me play, and he was convinced they would follow my playing with interest and offer me a hockey scholarship when the time was right. I told everyone, and for some reason, Felix got it into his head that he needed to call me future-NHL-Star-Shaun every time he spoke to me. Asshole.

Soren stood next to me and smoothed the arm of my suit. "It's fine."

I lifted my jacket. "But look how tight the pants are over my ass."

Felix snorted a laugh, but Soren shrugged. "Both my dads have that issue, comes with the hockey playing territory." Then, he offered Felix a hand to get up, and they snuck in a quick kiss.

"Photos here!" Mom made me pose at the bottom of the stairs—all I could think was that my pants were tight, the jacket gripped me like a glove, and the tie was going to kill me.

She was driving me to pick up Kenji, which meant more photos at Kenji's place, and Felix and

Soren split to head out to the school gym where the Junior Prom was all set up with some James Bond theme. Hence the dark suits.

I'd been practicing my Scottish accent for my best Sean Connery, but it was shit. I decided I was more Austin Powers, than James Bond, but whatever, Kenji would still smile at me.

I needed his smiles like I needed to breathe.

Kenji's sobo opened the door, stepping back to let me and Mom in, then we all waited, and I wondered where Kenji was, until I spotted him coming down the stairs, distracted by his watch, which he couldn't get to strap up.

He hadn't meant to make a rom-com entrance, but wow.

He wore a suit like I did, but his was this unstructured flowing drape of shiny black, over a shimmery pink shirt that was more Lycra than plain old cotton. It glittered under the lights, and when he got to the bottom of the stairs and had his watch fixed, he met my gaze, and jeez… his eyes were smoky with liner, his lashes long, his lips shiny with gloss, and I was gone.

I mean. Gone.

"Wow," I said because words failed me.

He blushed.. "Is it too extra?"

I think my mouth fell open. Too extra? My entire body hummed with how gorgeous he was.

"It's perfect. *You're* perfect."

Only, he dipped his head, and I could see the hint of fear in his expression.

"Are you okay?" I asked quietly.

He smiled up at me, then leaned there, all femme fatale. "You look so hot," he murmured, changing the subject.

But I wasn't going for being distracted, and everyone else in the hall, cameras out, talking, faded away. I took his arm and led him to the mirror and stood him in front of me. "Look at us," I said. "Together."

Kenji frowned, but his expression softened as I took his hand and placed our laced fingers over his heart.

"Perfect," he whispered.

I'd take that as a win because I was head over heels for Kenji Kelly, and he was my everything, and I would spend every hour thinking up ways to make him see how perfect we were. Starting tonight.

Kenji

Man, life sure was unpredictable.

If someone had pulled me aside a year ago and told me I wouldn't be skating anymore, and I would be dating Shaun Stanton, I would have laughed so hard I would have passed out.

Things sure could change with a little time and a lot of love.

Oh, and a dump truck full of chaos.

"Come stand here in front of the doorway," Mom called, taking Shaun by the arm, and dragging him into the living room. Well, he went willingly. Few people could move Shaun against his will, especially my little mother. Shaun's mom and mine positioned us by the bow window. The photo shoot was now underway. Sobo and Dad stood off to the side, smiling, and Koro sat atop the fireplace mantle glowering as we were blocking his favorite late afternoon nap spot.

"OKAY, NOW FACE EACH OTHER."

"Now stand back-to-back."

"Move to the left, Kenji."

"Put your arm around him, Shaun."

. . .

On and on it went, until Dad called an end to it. The moms began comparing images, then noting who wanted which ones.

"I have something for you both," Sobo said, shuffling up to us, her wrinkled hands clutching something. Shaun glanced down at me. I suspected I knew what was coming but held out my hand anyway. Shaun did the same. Tiny fabric pouches were placed in our palms. "Now you will have good luck and be protected. Put them in your pockets. Go ahead do so now."

We hurried to shove the omamori packets into our suit pockets.

"Arigato," Shaun said, then bowed to Sobo. He was working so hard to learn Japanese. So far, he knew thank you, goodbye, and damn cat. It was a work in progress.

"Hey, Kenji, can I get one minute before you leave?" Dad asked.

I nodded, then followed him into the backyard. The sun was setting, the days longer and warmer as May settled her warmth over the Keystone State.

"Okay, so a few things," he said, parking his butt

on the railing of our back porch. "One. No drinking and driving."

"Dad, no one in our group drinks," I reminded him.

"I know, but peer pressure. Just humor me and promise no booze."

"I promise," I vowed.

"Okay, two." He held up a pair of fingers. "I know you're renting a hotel room in town with the rest of your class tonight. Which will be fun. No one will have to be dead tired driving or worse. But that also opens up a different concern that your mom and I have."

He pulled two condoms in foil pouches from the back pocket of his jeans.

"Dad, oh my God!" I felt my face flame. "Put those away."

"Nope, sorry, you have to take them. Sobo gave you good luck charms to protect you. These will protect you in ways that the amulets she bought outside the Shinto temple yesterday when she visited can't."

"Dad, honestly, this is…" Words failed me, but I took the condoms and rushed to tuck them into my wallet. "Thanks."

"I know, it's embarrassing, but I also remember what it was like to be seventeen."

"Please, do not tell me about it." I waved a hand in the air, got a chuckle and a fast hug from my father, and then, went to find Shaun, who was having his tie fixed by his mother. Again.

"We good to go?" Shaun asked. I nodded, pecked my mother and grandmother on their cheeks, and went to the front door to find my dress shoes. I grabbed my overnight bag, which was waiting for me in the foyer.

"Everything okay with your dad?" Shaun asked as we climbed into the back seat of his mother's car.

"Yeah." I glanced out of the window to find Mrs. Stanton talking with my parents, all still on the sidewalk. We were now fashionably late. I texted the guys to let them know we were on the way, then glanced at Shaun. He had tugged his tie loose already. "So, my father gave me condoms for tonight." Shaun's blue eyes widened. "Right? But he's so straight he didn't think to add in some lube."

Shaun snorted, the pink in his cheeks the same color as the setting sun. "It's the thought that counts, right? That's what my mother says all the time."

"Yeah, I guess. I mean I get it, but…"

I let it drop. Mrs. Stanton was opening her car

door. And even though it was mortifying to the extreme to have your father give you condoms, it was meant with love. He had no way of knowing that Shaun and I were not at that place yet. We'd kissed, sure, sometimes real heavily, but he always drew back when things got too heated. He didn't want to push me. My being healthy mentally and physically was his number one concern, not the state of his dick. Totally Shaun. I adored him for it. I wasn't ready. Yet. But soon. My head was a much happier place now. The meds had been tweaked a few times, and I was feeling the best I had ever felt. Therapy, group, and family counseling were working. Yeah, I still had days where it was a huge struggle, but they were growing further apart. Knowing that Ilya was out of the country and never coming back helped. Russia would probably never extradite him. I prayed I never saw him coaching another young person.

"You okay?" Shaun asked, his hand coming to rest on my thigh.

"Yep, just thinking about stuff. And now, I'm putting that stuff into a box. Tonight is for us. Fun times await!"

Mrs. Stanton got us to the school without incident. Guess the good luck packets were working. We grabbed our bags, then Shaun kissed his mom goodbye. He took my hand in his as another car pulled up behind us, and Tyler and Jonah piled out.

"Man, talk about drip," I heard Soren call as he and Felix joined us.

Tyler gave me a hug, while Jonah, always with camera in hand, began snapping images of us, the campus, and the other kids filing into the gym in their suits and gowns. The night was sparkly, filled with promise and laughter.

"So, are we heading in or are we going to stand out here admiring ourselves?" Soren enquired, his arm resting around his boyfriend's shoulder.

I tipped my head. The sound of Dua Lipa's "Levitating" flowed out into the balmy night.

"Oh we are *so* going in!" I shouted as I grabbed my boyfriend's strong hand. His loving gaze fell to me, a smile pulling at his kissable lips.

With a hoot we rushed to the gym, the six of us, ready to face whatever the world held for us in senior year and beyond. Our futures had never looked brighter.

THE END

. . .

IF YOU OR SOMEONE YOU KNOW IS BATTLING AN eating disorder, please know that you are not alone.

You can find confidential help online at the National Alliance for Eating Disorders at https://www.allianceforeatingdisorders.com/

Harrisburg Railers

Owatonna U Hockey

Arizona Raptors

Boston Rebels

LA Storm

Chesterford Coyotes - Young Adult

Harrisburg Railers

When hockey wunderkind Tennant Rowe meets his new coach, he knows he's in trouble. Jared Madsen is nine years older than Tennant, impossibly attractive, and — worst of all — his brother's off-limits best friend. Is their chemistry worth the risk?

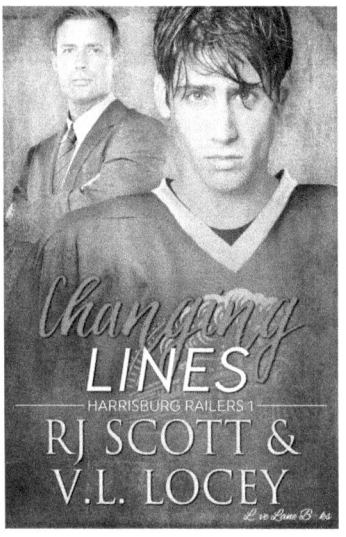

Changing Lines (Railers 1)

Can Tennant show Jared that age is just a number, and that love is all that matters?

The Rowe Brothers are famous hockey hotshots, but as the youngest of the trio, Tennant has always had to play against his brothers' reputations. To get out of their shadows, and against their advice, he accepts a trade to the Harrisburg Railers, where he runs into Jared Madsen. Mads is an old family friend and his brother's one-time teammate. Mads is Tennant's new coach. And Mads is the sexiest thing he's ever laid eyes on.

Jared Madsen's hockey career was cut short by a fault in his heart, but coaching keeps him close to the game. When Ten is traded to the team, his carefully organized world is thrown into chaos. Nine years his junior and his best friend's brother, he knows Ten is strictly off-limits, but as soon as he sees Ten's moves, on and off the ice, he knows that his heart could get him into trouble again.

Changing Lines

Harrisburg Railers (Hockey Romance)

1. Changing Lines
2. First Season
3. Deep Edge
4. Poke Check

5. Last Defense
6. Goal Line
7. Neutral Zone
8. Hat Trick
9. Save The Date
10. Baby Makes Three
11. Rivals
12. Perfect Gifts
13. Family First

Railers Volume 1 | Railers Volume 2 | Railers Volume 3 | Railers Volume 4

Owatonna U, College Hockey

Meet the men of Owatonna University's hockey team

Ryker (Owatonna U, 1)

Ryker

Ryker is hockey royalty, Jacob is a poor country boy. Can two vastly different people find common ground and become the men they want to be?

Ryker comes from a long line of championship-winning hockey players. Playing college hockey to develop his game is his only focus, and nothing will stand in the way of him working to become the best player. He has no room for relationships, people who point out his flaws, or anyone who calls him on his dreams. He certainly has no place for love, and meeting Jacob is nothing but a useful distraction on the side. After all trying to get his Owatonna Eagles teammate into bed is less work and more play. When tragedy rocks his family, his charmed life crumbles, and the only person he can turn to is the same one who claims to hate him.

Jacob Benson has only known hard work and stifling conservative values his whole life. Born and raised in the small rural community of Eden Crossing, Minnesota, he's the only son of a hard-working but struggling dairy farming family. Jacob is using his skills in hockey to finance his way to an agricultural science degree. These four years at Owatonna U. will probably be the only time he has to enjoy life, gain acceptance about his sexuality, and live openly before his inevitable return to the farm. Running into a pretty rich boy like Ryker Madsen is putting a damper on his enjoyment of life away from home. Ryker's flip, conceited, carefree attitude grates on Jacob's every nerve. So why, if Ryker is everything he dislikes, does he want nothing more than to explore the sinful dreams that his annoying teammate stars in every night?

Ryker

Owatonna U Hockey (Hockey Romance)

1. Ryker
2. Scott
3. Benoit
4. Christmas Lights
5. Valentine's Hearts
6. Desert Dreams

Coast to Coast (Arizona Raptors 1)

Coast To Coast

When opposites attract, this bottom-of-the-league team will never be the same again.

A stipulation in his father's will forces Mark back into the arms of a family that disowned him and leaves him one-third owner of a hockey team facing financial ruin. He doesn't even watch hockey, let alone like it, and wants nothing more than to head back to New York. Then there's the new coach, a stubborn, opinionated, irritating man with superiority issues and questionable music taste. Butting heads with Rowen becomes the new normal, but it comes with passionate debate and an all-consuming lust.

Challenged to rebuild one of the worst teams in the league into a future cup contender, Rowen can't pass up the opportunity. Never in his twenty years of hockey has he ever seen a team managed so badly or coached players overflowing with resentment and bigotry. Yet there's something about this team and this city that compels him to roll up his sleeves and start dismantling. If only Mark, one of three siblings who now own the Raptors, wasn't so damned rock-headed yet so damned appealing his job might be easier. It doesn't look like either is willing to give in, but one night in a dark, desert hotel changes everything.

Coast To Coast

Arizona Raptors (Hockey Romance)

1. Coast To Coast
2. Across the Pond
3. Shadow and Light

4. Sugar and Ice
5. School and Rock

Boston Rebels

Top Shelf (Boston Rebels 1)

Top Shelf

Acting on the attraction to his best friend's brother has
always been off the table for Xander until a passionate
hookup with Mason at a beach resort begins a love affair
that burns long after summer ends.

Mason specializes in assisting same-sex couples on their

journey to becoming parents and fighting every rule that blocks his way in the stuck-in-the-past agency that hired him. Living in his brother's pool house is rent-free, and every cent he earns he saves for his dream—that one day he'd have his own company helping others. The downside is that he has to see his annoying brother every day, the upside is that his brother's teammates from the Boston Rebels make regular visits. The eye candy that passes Mason's window is almost enough to make him consider dating a hockey player, but not just any player though. Ever since Xander—his brother's childhood friend—came out as gay at a press conference, Mason's puppy love has turned into a burning attraction he can no longer ignore.

Hockey has been one of Xander's main focuses since he was old enough to balance on skates. Well, hockey and Mason Kingsley, but Mason was always unattainable. Now that he's about to see thirty candles on his birthday cake and is no longer hiding the fact he's gay, he's ready to find a soul mate to make his life complete. A summer vacation is just what he needs to have time to think, but when the Boston Rebels arriving in paradise with Mason in tow, thinking is the last thing he needs. One torrid night under a balmy moon and rules about not messing with his best friend's brother vanish on a warm, tropical breeze.

Summer romances don't generally last past Labor Day, but with the new season about to begin Xander and Mason are going to have to face the world and decide if their love is real enough to withstand everything.

Boston Rebels

Lost In Boston (Free Prequel Novella)

1. Top Shelf
2. Back Check
3. Snowed
4. Royal Lines
5. Blade
6. Rental

LA Storm

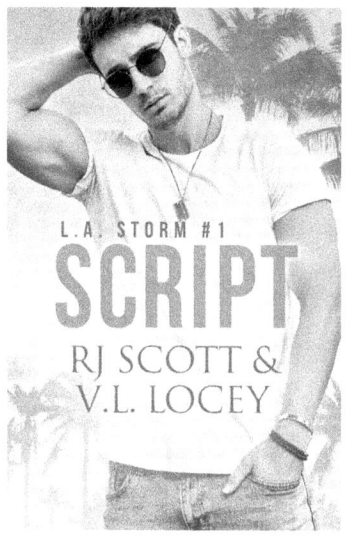

Script (LA Storm, 1)

Script

Hollywood A-lister Finn might be Canadian, but he needs Cameron to show him how to hockey.

Actor Finn Kerrigan is at a crossroads. After growing up a soap star, then starring in a hugely successful trilogy of action movies, he's finally given the chance to read a heartfelt and passionate script that could change his life forever. The role would be enough for people to see him as a serious actor, and maybe even win him an award or two (and no, a golden raspberry award for his action movies doesn't count). Once established as a serious actor he's sure he can come out of the closet and finally live his truth.

When he lies to get the part of a hockey player on a struggling team, he suddenly has nowhere to hide. He might be Canadian, but the last time he skated he was ten, and no, he doesn't have hockey in his blood. With only a month until filming starts, he about to be exposed, but partnered with a player who's supposed to be giving him tips, he doesn't realize how many of his secrets will come to light. Falling in lust, one heated kiss at a time, is inevitable, but giving Cameron up at the end of the shoot could break his heart.

Cameron Chavkin is the face of the LA Storm. And the body, and the hair, and the smile. He's at the prime of his career, men and women want to be with him, and he's skating better than he ever has before. His house sits next to a famous rock star's mansion, his garage is filled with expensive cars, and he's even been asked to mentor a once-famous actor in a new hockey movie. Life is pretty sweet. Until the bad boy of hockey meets Finn, a man on the edge with more secrets than Cameron has endorsements. Knowing better than to get involved, Cameron is swept up despite himself, and when it's time to say goodbye to the

Storm's most eligible bachelor is finding it hard to follow the script.

Script

LA Storm

1. Script
2. Second
3. Shield
4. Spiral

Also By RJ Scott

For a full list of ebooks and links please scan the code
above or visit rjscott.co.uk/rjbooks

Meet RJ Scott

RJ discovered romance in books at a very young age and realized that if there wasn't romance on the page, she could create it in her head. With over one hundred and fifty books published, she is a full time author of gay romance.

She lives and works out of her home in the beautiful English countryside, spends her spare time reading, watching films, and enjoying time with her family.

The last time she had a week's break from writing she didn't like it one little bit and has yet to meet a box of chocolates she couldn't defeat.

www.rjscott.co.uk | rj@rjscott.co.uk

NEWSLETTER - rjscott.co.uk/rjnews

facebook.com/author.rjscott

x.com/Rjscott_author

instagram.com/rjscott_author

amazon.com/author/rj-scott

bookbub.com/authors/rj-scott

goodreads.com/rjscott

pinterest.com/rjscottauthor

Also By VL Locey

For a full list of ebooks and links please scan the code above or visit vllocey.com/stories-from-vl-locey

Meet V.L. Locey

V.L. Locey loves worn jeans, yoga, belly laughs, walking, reading and writing lusty tales, Greek mythology, the New York Rangers, comic books, and coffee.

(Not necessarily in that order.)

She shares her life with her husband, her daughter, one dog, two cats, a flock of assorted domestic fowl, and two Jersey steers.

When not writing spicy romances, she enjoys spending her day with her menagerie in the rolling hills of Pennsylvania with a cup of fresh java in hand.

vllocey.com
vicki@vllocey.com

Newsletter - vllocey.com/newsletter

facebook.com/V.L.Locey

x.com/vllocey

instagram.com/vl_locey

bookbub.com/authors/v-l-locey

goodreads.com/vllocey

pinterest.com/vllocey